Love Tools

Bluestone Series: Book One

Isobel Reed

The characters and events in this book are fictitious. Any similarity to real persons, living or dead, places, or events is coincidental and not intended by the author.

If you purchase this book without a cover you should be aware that this book may have been stolen property and reported as "unsold and destroyed" to the publisher. In such case the author has not received any payment for this "stripped book."

Love Tools: Bluestone Series: Book One
Copyright © 2022 Isobel Reed
All rights reserved.

ISBN: (print) 978-1-958136-33-1
(ebook) 978-1-958136-21-8

Inkspell Publishing
207 Moonglow Circle #101
Murrells Inlet, SC 29576

Cover art by: Fantasia Frog Designs
Edited by: Yezanira Venecia

DEDICATION

For my family. Thank you for all the love and support you have given me. And for not complaining (much) when I make you read my stories.

ISOBEL REED

CHAPTER ONE

Lily stared at the boarded-up windows and took a deep breath. There was no turning back now. Pulling the keys from her handbag, she unlocked the door and followed the creak into the dimly lit store.

To her surprise the shelves were still stocked and brimming with power tools, each item covered in a layer of dust that had already started to make its way up her nostrils.

"What the hell are you doing here, Lily," she muttered to herself as she ran her fingers across the counter.

It was going to be more work than she ever imagined to get this place up and running. She just hoped the apartment upstairs was in better condition.

After exploring the shop floor, she went to find out. She followed the beige hallway into the living room, took a seat on the squeaky leather sofa, and looked around. The space was depressing, habitable but depressing nonetheless. How could her dad have lived here for so long and it still feel so empty?

Furniture was sparse, other than the chair she sat in, the only other items that remained were a flatscreen TV, a scratched wooden coffee table and a small shelving unit scattered with a few books and a couple of picture frames.

She looked over at the kitchen adjoining the living room and noticed some basic appliances. It felt strange to be in his space. His home. Surrounded by his things. Was there a right way to feel?

No. He's nothing to you; he made damn sure of that. Suck it up and do what you need to do.

Taking off her jacket, she started to gather up her wild blonde hair and tied it on top of her head. It was time to get to work.

With the boxes in sight already full, she reached for some rubbish bags and began filling them with his things. She threw in every frame she came across, not ready to look at pictures of him yet.

Once she'd made it into the bedroom, she went straight to the wardrobe at the bottom of the bed. Without taking the time to examine the clothes that still hung there, she quickly scooped up the hangers and filled her bag.

It wasn't long until black sacks lined the hallway. But she wasn't ready to throw them out quite yet. She pondered if there might be a time in the near future that she would feel strong enough to sit down and go through all of his things.

I should just burn them.

Ignoring the new urge to set fire to everything that reminded her of Matthew, she let out a big sigh and picked up her luggage. The fate of the belongings would have to wait while she concentrated on unpacking her own stuff.

After emptying her suitcases, she was still full of energy. Itching to make a start on the store, she frantically searched the cupboards for cleaning products, finding enough to at least make a dent. For the sake of her bank balance, she needed to get this place open as quickly as possible. Changing into some old clothes she didn't mind getting dirty, she readied herself for just one of the many challenges that lay ahead.

Downstairs, she peered at the grimy surfaces and realised that every nook and cranny would need her attention. Deciding against removing all the stock before she launched into cleaning, she instead chose to do one shelf at a time. After setting a goal for at least one aisle before bed, she needed some inspiration. It was time for a little mood music. Reaching for her phone and speakers, she selected her favourite playlist and turned up the volume.

Swaying to the rhythm, she sang along and emptied each shelf before working her domestic magic. Every wipe down gave her a sense of achievement, she even started to believe that maybe things would be okay after all.

Distracted by a particularly upbeat song, she felt herself get lost in the music, her mood lifting with every hip shake. It wasn't long before she was in a world of her own and busting out moves all along the shop floor.

That was until a loud, very forced cough from behind scared the living daylights out of her. Quickly twisting around, she placed a hand over her heart, which felt like it was about to jump right out of her chest, and was met with an inquisitive, blue-eyed stare. A man with an amused smirk pasted on his face was casually slouched against an empty shelf. A tall, dark-haired man who couldn't be much older than her.

Still in shock, a barrage of cursing ensued before she was finally able to string a sentence together.

"You scared the hell out of me!" She angrily put a stop to the music. "Who are you? How did you get in here?" Alarm bells sounded as she realised she was all alone with a strange man.

Shit. Stranger danger.

Trying to mask any fear, she crossed her arms defiantly and offered up her scariest scowl.

Yeah, that'll stop him from murdering you.

"Well hello to you too." The man began to straighten himself. "I might ask you the very same question. Who are you, darlin', and how did *you* get in here?" His deep, gravelly voice sent a shiver down her spine.

The more she studied him, the more self-conscious she became, so much so that she found herself tugging down her shorts and vest.

"I own this place. This *locked* store. How did *you* get in here?"

"You *own* this place?" He scrunched up his face, as if confused. "That's not possible. This place hasn't been on the market."

"Well, it clearly *is* possible cos it's mine." Who did this guy think he was?

He pulled out a set of keys from his denim pocket and dangled them in front of her. "Look, I was a friend of Matt's, and I know for a fact this place wasn't up for sale."

Her patience was beginning to wane. Of course Matt hadn't mentioned her—why would he? Selfish bastard was probably all too aware of the reaction he would have faced. Any fear she might have had quickly switched back to rage. A rage that apparently gave her the balls to snatch the keys right out of the man's hands.

"Matthew was my dad. And my *dad* left me this place in his will."

The man, still staring at his empty hand, was quiet for a moment while he processed what she'd just barked at him. Lily took the opportunity to scan his face and let her eyes wander down him. His broad shoulders filled out his check shirt that pulled tight across his muscled chest. She tried her hardest not to gawk as her gaze travelled down farther to his mud-stained denim jeans that moulded perfectly to tensed thighs.

Holy shit, he's hot. Do all the men in Montana look like this?

"You about done checking me out, darlin', or do you want me to turn around and show you the back?"

She felt her cheeks flame as her eyes flicked back up and she caught sight of his cocky grin. Before she could attempt to deny what she'd been doing, his expression turned more serious as he gave her a once-over. "I didn't know Matt had a daughter."

Surprise, surprise.

"No shit. He wasn't exactly father of the year."

Lily couldn't help but think of the irony. Her father had become friends with some guy young enough to be his son, yet he still couldn't quite be bothered to pick up the phone and call his own daughter.

Marlboro Man's smile became crooked as his glare intensified. "You always swear like a trucker, darlin'? Here I thought English women were all class and manners."

Is he being fucking serious?

She let out a huff; she couldn't believe the nerve of this guy. "I'm sorry, have I stepped into the past? Are you gonna ask me why a little woman like me isn't married next?"

"All right, sweetheart, calm down." He sniggered, clearly amused by the steam coming out of her ears.

Stepping closer to him, she tilted her head up to meet his gaze. "I'm not, nor will I ever, be your *sweetheart*. Now, if you don't mind, you need to get the hell out of my store before I call the police."

Laughing, he threw his hands up in the air in mercy, a smile still glued to his face. "Whatever you say, *sweetheart*."

***

Lily steered her cart into the cleaning aisle. Opting for the cheapest items, she began to fill her trolley, still daunted by what she'd taken on.

As she made her way to the checkout, she could feel the curiosity from each local she passed. Bluestone County was a small town, nothing like London. She certainly wouldn't have the anonymity she had back home.

Despite the whispers following her around the supermarket, she was pleased that she'd managed to avoid any interrogations, although she had no doubt they were coming.

As she carried her shopping back down the cobblestone streets, a high-pitched voice rang out behind her.

"Need some help?"

She turned to see a wiry, denim-clad woman peering

over at her. Long, straight auburn hair framed her heart-shaped face that displayed a friendly, wide-eyed smile. Lily guessed they were around the same age. She politely declined the woman's help, but before she could continue on her way, the woman spoke again.

"You're Matt's daughter, right? You're staying at the store?"

One person. She'd told one person. How had news travelled so fast?

"Um. Yeah. How did you …?"

"Oh, it's a small town." She giggled before putting out her hand to introduce herself. "I'm Sam."

Lily freed up a hand and shook it. "Lily, nice to meet you."

"Wow, that accent is awesome. You sound like something out of that TV show, *Downton Abbey*." Before Lily could decide if that was a compliment or an insult, Sam grabbed one of the bags out of her hand and motioned for Lily to follow her. "Here, I'll help. I'm heading that way anyway."

With no choice but to follow, Lily hurried to catch up, her feet dodging uneven cobbles as they continued their walk toward the shop.

"So, ya gonna reopen it? The store, I mean?"

"Hopefully. It needs a good clean. I also need to familiarise myself with the products. Who knew there were so many different types of drills?"

Sam let out a chuckle. "So I take it you're gonna keep it as a hardware store?" Her eyes roved over Lily as if trying to work something out.

"Yeah, why?" Lily suddenly felt defensive. Was it so odd she was going to be selling tools? What else was she supposed to do with it? It made sense to keep it as it was. Besides, she had the stock. And no other ideas. Or money.

"Just curious. I guess most folks would take one look at you and assume you would try and turn it into something girly, like a clothing boutique or a cake shop."

Girly? That's a first.

"Well, sorry to disappoint, but I can't bake, and I know even less about fashion than power drills, so I think I'm just gonna have to stick to selling tools."

Sam burst into laughter just before they reached the store. "Damn, girl. I like you. You've got some spunk. Y'know, I own a ranch, just outside of town. I got a lot of my equipment from Matt's, back in the day. I'd be happy to show you some of them, if you want to come on out? Y'know, so you can get a feel for what the products do."

"Really?" Lily already knew she needed all the help she could get. "Um … that would actually be really useful."

"Cool. Let's swap numbers and I'll text you the address."

After numbers were exchanged and a day for the visit was agreed, Sam left Lily to get on with her to-do list. But before Lily could even wipe down a surface, her phone rang—it was her mum again. After letting out a huge sigh, she reluctantly answered.

Her mother immediately launched back into a tirade. Apparently, this morning's talking to wasn't enough. Or last night's. Or the one she had to endure on the ride over to the airport.

"It's just not like you, Lily. To be this reckless. When are you going to come to your senses and come back home?"

Lily took a seat behind the counter; she knew that this was going to be a long one. "Mum, please. I can't keep having the same conversation with you."

"So, what, you're just gonna follow in your father's footsteps now? Abandon your family, your friends, your life? And for what, a silly store in the middle of nowhere?"

Lily studied the shop floor that lay ahead of her. She wasn't completely sure why, but she knew in her heart that Bluestone was where she needed to be. Unfortunately, a feeling in her gut was proving difficult to explain to her mother.

"I don't expect you to understand, Mum. And I'm not abandoning you or Alice, I just don't have anything back home, you know, to keep me there."

"So, your own mother and sister aren't enough for you?"

Wow. She was laying it on thick today. She knew for a fact that Alice supported her. Yes, as half-sisters go, they were pretty close. But unlike her mother, her sister just wanted Lily to be happy. Even if that did mean moving halfway across the world.

Lily was already sick of being made to feel guilty. "You've both got people you love, Mum, and jobs that you actually enjoy. I don't have that. I don't want to work in a dead-end job for the rest of my life. I mean, I was an admin assistant for God's sake, with no possible prospects. Out here, I'm a business owner."

"Your dad's business." Her mother sneered.

"So what? I don't care that it was his. It's the least he could do for me, don't you think?"

The line went quiet for a while and Lily could feel herself getting frustrated.

"I know, Lily. I just don't get why you have to move there. Sell the business and use the money to do something over here. You don't have to leave the country because you're single, darling. There are plenty of men here in London. In fact, I was talking to Julie the other day and her son just moved back over from Dubai. You remember Tom, don't you? Very handsome. And completely rolling in it. He was asking about you. I told Julie that she should give him your number."

Oh my freaking God, you've got to be kidding me?

Lily's head dropped to the counter. It was going to be a long day.

***

Despite the store clean-up going well, being in one place for so long was beginning to get to Lily. She was guessing that talking to only herself and her mother for a whole week was likely the culprit, so visiting Sam's ranch was a welcome relief.

It was a warm, sunny day, and she was looking forward to spending it outdoors. Not knowing what you were supposed to wear on a ranch tour, she'd resisted the urge to wear flip-flops and paired her jeans and vest combo with boots.

Quietly congratulating herself for her outfit choice, she pulled up outside the main house. She couldn't quite believe the size of the land surrounding her. Climbing out of the car, she felt the fresh air fill her lungs as she continued to survey what looked like miles and miles of fields.

While she was taking in the view, Sam came into sight and shouted over to her. Pleased to see a friendly face, Lily waved and started toward her.

"Come in, come in," Sam excitedly greeted.

Following Sam into the house, Lily was stunned at just how grand it was. To the left of the hall was a large, modern living room with three navy sofas and a giant television. Sam then led her through the room and into an equally as impressive kitchen, complete with stainless steel appliances and a huge breakfast bar with silver stools scattered around it.

"Wow, this place is amazing. How long have you lived here?"

"Actually, I grew up here. It didn't always look like this though, trust me. It needed a lot of updating, so my brother and I spent a lot of time … and money fixing it up a couple of years ago."

"Well, you guys did good. This is like my dream kitchen." Lily ran her hands over the granite surfaces.

"Thank you." A shy smile appeared on Sam's face as she poured them some juice. "Hopefully, you'll like the rest of the place too."

"Oh, I have no doubt," Lily assured her.

After Sam went into more detail about the refurbishment the house had undergone, they took a stroll outside, through the patio doors and into her yard, which was pretty much just another field.

Leading Lily over to what looked like a cross between a tractor and a quad bike, Sam gestured her inside. After clambering in, Sam announced that they were now ready to explore the rest of the ranch.

The stables were the first stop of the tour, which ironically were within walking distance to the house.

"You have so many," Lily exclaimed on her way over to pet the silky-smooth skin of the first horse poking its head toward her.

"Yeah, it's a big source of our income. We house a few of them for their owners and offer up training and riding lessons." Sam gently stroked the mane of an affectionate chestnut horse.

"They're so beautiful. I might have to take one of your lessons."

"I'd be happy to give you a freebie. Having another woman around here would be a welcome relief from all the testosterone floating about."

Lily giggled. It dawned on her that Sam was probably just in much need of a friend as she was.

The next stop on the tour was the guest cabins, which were rented out to tourists looking for authentic country experiences. Sam explained that it was called a "dude ranch." From what Lily understood, people from all over America would come stay out there for a week and learn to ride, fish and go on hikes.

Wandering around one of the cabins, Lily could see the appeal. It was all self-contained, nicely decorated and benefited from a breathtaking view of the rolling hills. She wouldn't mind treating herself to a weekend here once she'd sorted out the store.

"How do you manage to do this and all the lessons and stuff?" She was exhausted at just the thought of it. Just maintaining the land had to be a full-time job, let alone having guests, training horses and teaching people how to ride.

Sam snorted at that. "It's not just me. I run the ranch

with my brother, Jake, and we've got ranch hands, a chef, the works. Come on, I'll take you to meet Jake."

Back in the vehicle, they drove through a collection of trees and into another field. She could make out a figure in the distance, fiddling with what looked like a fence.

It wasn't until they had parked next to the gate that Lily recognised Jake, having only recently kicked him out of the store. She started to feel nervous. Of all the men in Bluestone County, why did this one have to be Sam's brother?

CHAPTER TWO

As if by magic, there she was. He looked up to see the woman he'd spent the past week thinking about, and she was even more beautiful than he'd remembered. This time her long, wavy, golden hair was down, shimmering in the sun and swaying along with the breeze. She wore a simple tank top that clung to all her delicious curves and tight, dark, denim jeans that he swore looked like they were painted on, not that he was complaining.

He felt himself grin during Sam's introduction, which allowed him to finally put a name to that pretty face. Lily. Lily who was fidgeting and fumbling with her fingers. He could tell she was just as unprepared to see him as he was to see her. Nervous even.

Don't be an asshole, Jake.

"Let me guess, you're here to kick me off my own land now too?"

Damnit.

"Funny. No, just getting the tour from your lovely sister. You sure you're related?" she sarcastically replied.

There was the sass he remembered. "Ouch. I see there's been no attitude adjustment since we last met, huh?"

What are you, five? You gonna pull her hair next?

17

"Be nice Jake," Sam piped.

Clicking his tongue, he ignored his sister and stared into Lily's emerald eyes once again; they were even more mesmerizing in the sunlight.

"Sorry, I'm not enough of a lady for you, *sweetheart*." Her attempted scowl was almost cute.

"I'd be more than happy to teach you some manners, darlin'." He winked.

Deep down he knew that he shouldn't be trying to provoke her, but he couldn't help himself. Seeing the fire in her eyes did something to him that he couldn't explain. Even watching her try to snarl at him was making him feel funny.

"Okay, you two"—Sam put on her teaching voice— "play nice. Let's go get some lunch and cool off. Ryan's probably cooked up a feast."

"I'll join you," Jake announced, trying not to laugh at Lily's horrified reaction.

He'd finished mending the fence and he wasn't about to let this opportunity pass him by.

After gathering up his tools, he headed over to the ATV they arrived on. It was a two-seater, so when Lily realised she'd have to sit on his lap during the ride back, he couldn't help but grin at her dramatic reaction. He considered being a gentleman for a moment and walking back, but this was more fun. As he guided her onto his lap, he took way too much pleasure in pressing her warm, soft skin against him as he settled his hands around her waist. She felt so damn good.

Don't be a pervert, man, think about something else, anything else.

But he couldn't. If he thought he wanted her before, five minutes of her body being pressed against his only solidified those feelings.

***

Jake's stomach growled at the smell of gravy as they

walked into the on-site restaurant. Sam was right; Ryan had cooked up a feast. Even after all the guests were full, there was plenty to go around. Having not eaten since five, Jake eagerly filled his plate and took a seat with their ranch hands, Duke and Brody.

Their restaurant was cafeteria-style: on the right there were tables dotted around the windows and on the left there was one long counter where guests could help themselves to plates, cutlery and food. Ryan had been begging for a properly equipped kitchen for years, and it made sense to build one for him with a seating area attached. Now they had a place for guests to eat whatever the weather, and it meant they could open the ranch to year-round guests.

As Duke and Brody talked, Jake kept one eye on Lily. She was sitting with Sam and Ryan just a few tables away. As she let out a giggle and pushed Ryan with one hand, Jake was taken aback by the sudden wave of jealousy that came over him. Was she interested in Ryan? Annoyed at just how much he cared, he made his way over to them to see for himself.

Setting down his plate at their table, he felt the atmosphere change. Lily was the one staring at him, though, unable to mask her aversion to his presence.

"You know, Jake, I'm surprised you don't have a female chef working here. What with a woman's place being in the kitchen and all?" A wry smile lit up her eyes as she looked to him, daring him to say something.

Ryan and Sam remained silent, exchanging looks.

So she wanted another round? He was more than willing to oblige.

"Well, men are better at most things, I guess, even cooking." He grinned, their gazes still entwined as he placed a forkful of food in his mouth.

Clearing his throat and looking sheepish, Ryan excused himself. Sam quickly followed, clearly not wanting any part in this conversation either.

"Wow, you really are an arsehole, aren't you?"

Jake watched as Lily shook her head in irritation.

"So, back to cursing, huh? Interesting."

"Not classy enough for you?"

"What exactly is your problem with me?" Even though he liked the fire he stoked in her, he didn't want her to hate him. That was not part of the plan at all.

Wait. We have a plan?

She simply scoffed. "You mean I'm the only person who hasn't found your arrogance charming?"

"Oh, I'm all charm and then some, sweetheart." He winked. "If you ever feel like going for a … ride. Then I'd be more than happy to show you."

Shit. Now I'm an asshole and a pervert.

But it was too late. Lily let out a disgruntled huff, swiftly pushed back against the table, stood and walked away. And he couldn't even stop himself from watching.

***

Just days after he very nearly had hot gravy poured over his head, Jake was ready to try again. When he arrived at Matt's old store, Lily and Sam had already started clearing the entrance. Today was the day the boards on the windows were finally coming down, and he was here to help.

"Afternoon, all!" Jake bellowed out as he sauntered through the shop door.

Clearly not expecting him, he watched Lily immediately look to Sam for an explanation.

"Don't get mad. But Duke couldn't make it, so Jake agreed to step in and help. Wasn't that nice of him?" Sam half smiled over at her.

"Yeah, Lily, wasn't that nice of me?" Jake teased.

Even though he enjoyed watching her squirm, a little guilt leaked out as her features softened. He noticed a sense of resignation move over her.

"I'll go make us some coffees," Lily quietly announced before disappearing into the back room, leaving him alone with his sister's glare.

A minute later, Lily re-emerged, looking more like herself.

"Is it safe to drink?" Jake looked cautiously over at her as she passed him his mug.

"Don't worry, I'm not gonna poison you *before* I get my new windows, am I?" Lily assured him.

"Good to know." He flashed her his biggest smile before taking his drink outside to survey the boards.

He set his cup on the ground, then examined the board fixtures near the entrance, and then might have accidentally overheard Sam and Lily's conversation. What wasn't an accident though was leaning in closer so he could hear better.

"I'm sorry. Please don't be mad at me," Sam exclaimed, clearly talking about his presence.

"It's okay, really. I need the help, right? Plus, he's your brother, and if we're gonna hang out, I guess I need to learn to get along with him."

So, she wanted to try and get along? He definitely wasn't expecting that. Something in him shifted then. Suddenly feeling more motivated, he got to work.

Ten minutes later Sam joined him, and they got into a good rhythm. After getting one board down, he peered into the now very large hole in the wall and caught sight of Lily, who was restocking the shelves, swaying to music blasting into her headphones. Unable to look away, he studied every swing, captivated by the way she moved those hips.

He found himself smiling as she squinted over at him. Sunlight glowing across her angelic face as her body came to a standstill. Motioning toward her headphones, she quickly removed one of them and threw him a quizzical look.

"No dance show today?" he shouted over at her.

"You're hilarious." She pouted before placing her earphone back in.

Laughing to himself as he left her all riled up, he pulled

himself away and headed over to the remaining board and got to work.

Just as the last board came down, Sam received word from the ranch that one of the guests had requested a last-minute riding lesson. Pleasing the guests was their top priority. Happy guests meant good reviews and repeat business. After promising his sister he would stay and help Lily and definitely not antagonise her, she hurriedly made her way back.

When he ventured inside to tell Lily exactly why his sister had left, she didn't bother to hide her discomfort at being left alone with him. Now he really did feel bad. He wasn't an idiot. If ever there was an opportunity to change their relationship, it was now. Maybe he could even charm her. But before he could think of anything smooth to say, "You don't like me much, huh?" tumbled off his tongue.

The air went quiet while Lily deliberated her answer.

"I don't know you well enough not to like you."

That was a surprise. A good one. There was hope. At least he hadn't completely ruined his chances with her back at the ranch. Feeling his muscles start to unstiffen, he readied himself to try this again.

"I'll wait for the guys with the glass to come, see if they need any help."

Lily shuffled her feet, still looking uneasy. "Thank you for helping to take down the boards. I appreciate it. You don't have to wait for the window fitters, though, if you've got stuff to do?" The hint of vulnerability in her voice stirred something inside of him.

"You're welcome." He stared into her piercing green eyes, hoping to get her to look back into his. "I'm happy to stick around, make sure it all goes smoothly—it's no bother."

She nodded as a flush started to rise up her neck.

Damn, she's cute when she gets all shy.

The thought that she was shy had never occurred to him before. It certainly hadn't felt that way when she was busting his balls.

"Um. Can I get you another coffee, or I think I have some biscuits upstairs?" Her voice was shaky as she waved toward the back.

Wait. Do I make her nervous?

He instantly regretted agreeing to another cup after it meant her vanishing into the back room again. This new, coy side of her was intriguing. He started to wonder if her fiery demeanour had all been a front, some sort of defence mechanism.

Returning with two hot mugs of coffee, she gently handed him his drink. He felt an instant spark as her hand grazed his, so much so his eyes shot up to meet her equally as startled gaze.

"Son of a bitch" quietly slipped from her lips, causing him to chuckle.

"What?"

"Fuck. Sorry. I wasn't calling you a …" She trailed off, clearly flustered.

"It's okay. I have a feeling I'd know if it was directed at me." He offered up his warmest smile in an attempt to try and make her feel at ease. "So, what's your story?"

"My story?" With nowhere else to sit, she perched on the countertop.

"Yeah, your story. Moving to Bluestone to open a hardware store in your five-year plan?"

She let out an adorable girly giggle. It made him feel almost proud that he'd been the reason for it. "No, not exactly. Just time for a change I guess."

"That's it? You move thousands of miles away, just for a change?" He wasn't buying it. There was much more to this story.

Don't push her. She's finally let down some of her defences.

She took a sip of her drink, and, for a moment, she looked as though she'd slipped into a daydream. "Yep. I just needed something else, you know? Something was missing."

"And you think you'll find it here?"

"I hope so."

Before he could ask her the million questions he'd just thought of, the windows arrived, and they were back to work.

***

Two days after helping Lily out at the store, it was time for the ranch's weekly barbecue. Currently in full swing, guests had been filling up on burgers and beers for the past hour while he was buttering up their latest group of ladies. The oldest of which had taken a shine to him.

Flirting with Jean was a welcome distraction. After Sam had informed him she'd invited Lily, he'd been looking over at the house for the past hour, hoping to catch a glimpse of her.

As the ladies giggled, the mouth-watering aroma hit him once again. He'd still not eaten, and he could feel his belly start to grumble. Just as he was planning his escape, his eyes darted toward the house again. This time Lily was there, the sun setting behind her, as she made her way through the grass toward Sam.

Feeling his pulse quicken, food suddenly became the last thing on his mind. Feet frozen in place; he stole glances at her across the fire. Every time he caught her eye, he felt his stomach twinge. It was becoming abundantly clear that this wasn't just a crush. He wanted her. He wanted to make her his.

Once he'd finally excused himself from the group, Jake made a beeline for Sam and Lily. But as he crept up behind them, he heard his sister mention their dad, causing his footsteps to falter. Sam was telling her about their father passing. Now wasn't the time to think about that though, not today. Pushing away painful memories before they had a chance to surface, he took a deep breath and planted himself in front of them. Effectively ending their conversation.

"The guests are happy; I think we can let Ryan go for the night." He tried his hardest to focus on Sam, even as he felt Lily's eyes on him.

"Good idea," Sam agreed. After glancing back over at the table, his sister's smile widened as she turned back to him. "I think Jean has taken a shine to you."

Amused that she'd noticed, he let out a knowing laugh. Lily, on the other hand, let out a snort.

"And what's so funny about that? I'm a pretty charming guy, remember?"

"Oh, I remember." Lily turned around to face Sam. "Jean's the one with the glasses, right? Hmm ... maybe she needs a new prescription?"

"Wow," he tutted and shook his head, "and to think I was starting to like you."

"Oh, no, what a shame." Lily rolled her eyes.

Intervening, Sam abruptly stood up. "Okay, okay, you guys. Try and behave while I go speak to Ryan."

Letting out a huff, Jake took Sam's seat around the fire. Lily expertly ignored his gaze and presence and simply delved back into her burger. It only seemed to make him like her more.

As he took the sight of her in, he noticed her skin begin to goosebump. That was enough to propel him into action. Despite the pleasing sight of her in just shorts and a flimsy top, he didn't want her to catch a cold. That would not do at all.

Out of his seat, he wasted no time returning to the house, trying his best to remember where Sam kept all the blankets. After scanning the laundry cupboards, he eventually came across something to keep Lily warm.

Minutes later, he was back in front of her and passing over a shaggy blanket. Catching her baffled expression, he blurted out, "So you don't get cold."

She suspiciously accepted it as if it were a trick. "Um, thank you."

"You don't have to act so shocked. Believe it or not, I'm

a nice guy."

A gentle smile lit up her face as she motioned for him to take a seat next to her.

"So, Mr Nice Guy, you think you have a shot with Jean?"

Laughing, Jake reached for a beer in the cooler next to him. "I think Jean is way out of my league."

"I don't know, I reckon you could win her over with that charm of yours."

CHAPTER THREE

Lily had been in Bluestone almost two weeks now and it was safe to say the town was growing on her. It helped greatly that she'd actually made a friend. A friend that she could grab food with every now and again, which was exactly what she was doing.

Sam and Lily sat in the café opposite the store, where she'd become a regular given her supreme lack of cooking skills. Resting on the red cushioned steel chair, Lily slurped what was left of her strawberry milkshake, waiting for Sam to reply.

"Come on. Duke asked you out and you haven't answered him because?" Lily tried again.

"I just don't know." Sam threw her hands up in frustration before slumping her elbows back onto the table. "I like him, but I've known him forever. What if it's just a convenience thing? Like, I go out with him just because there's no one else?"

"It doesn't sound like that's the case, Sam. It actually sounds as though you've liked each other for a while but you're holding back for some reason. And I don't buy the convenience thing—I think you're wary cos you're his boss."

For some reason Lily loved giving out dating advice. She was even good at it. Plus, not having any kind of love life of her own allowed her to live vicariously through her friends.

"Maybe." Sam pushed what was left of her food around the plate. "Yeah. I think you're right. It would be weird, right?"

"No, not at all. Guys do it all the time, just cos you're a woman doesn't make it any different. If he doesn't care, then you shouldn't care either. Also, I think you make a cute couple."

"I still don't know; I just need to think about it some more." She downed what was left of her coke and settled her gaze on Lily. "Okay, enough about me. I haven't heard one thing about you. You're single, right?"

"Yes, I'm single. And there is honestly nothing to tell." Lily shook her head, thinking back to the last date she went on. "There are three types of guys that I attract: liars, cheaters and sociopaths. Hence, why I'm done with dating."

They both started to laugh. She'd found a kindred spirit in Sam; their friendship made a new life in Bluestone County less scary.

After she went on to describe some of her funnier dates, Sam had an idea.

"I'll tell you what, I'll go on a date with Duke … *if* you come with me?"

"What?! Like a chaperone?"

"No, like a double date."

Lily could feel her mouth hang open in horror; dating was the last thing she wanted to do. "Umm … what part of *I don't date* didn't you get? I'm not looking to meet anyone right now, Sam, especially with everything going on with the store. I need to concentrate on opening and making some money."

"Okay, but what if it's after the store opening? As a sort of celebration dinner. Please, please, please! I will owe you one. Please?"

Lots more begging ensued, pulling on her heartstrings.

Sam eventually wore her down. Lily, not expecting anything romantic to come of it, figured if anything she could do with making more friends in town.

***

Three weeks of cleaning, fixing and bartering had come down to today. Lily was finally ready to open the store. Excitedly, she inspected the shop floor one last time before unlocking the door. All she had to do now was wait.

The chair behind the counter proved beneficial as time ticked on without a single customer in sight. She started to think she'd gone about this all wrong. Word of mouth clearly hadn't worked. Maybe she should have tried something else, she wondered.

Three hours in, she had resorted to making up games to entertain herself. The door creaked open just as she let out a congratulatory cheer for making her latest shot in the bin.

"Not interrupting anything, am I?" Jake smirked as he swaggered over to her.

Perfect. Jake gets a front-row seat to my humiliation. And for fucks sake, why does he have to look so damn good today?

She let out a sigh as she slumped onto the counter. "No, not interrupting anything in fact. It's been dead all morning."

"Well, if that's how you greet all your customers I'm not surprised."

Was he really going to kick her while she was down? She thought they'd turned a corner, that night at the barbecue. "What do you want, Jake?" Lily puffed as she looked back into those dangerous blue eyes.

"I'm actually here to shop. I need some wire for one of the fences."

That perked her up. A sale was a sale. Now all she had to do was be nice. After rushing off to grab some wire, she handed it over and escorted him back to the till to ring it up.

With her friendliest smile, Lily passed him over his

change. "I never thought I'd say this, but … thank you—please come again."

"You must be desperate if you're asking me to come back." He laughed.

"I am," she admitted. "Look around, this place isn't exactly bustling."

She could see the pity take over his face. "I think I can help. Let me take you to lunch across the road—we can brainstorm a few ideas?"

"Really?" Maybe they had turned a corner after all. The few times she'd seen him since the barbecue, he had been making much more of an effort to talk to her and his teasing had become more playful than offensive. Even so, she couldn't help but feel wary. "You'd do that, even though I called you a wanker?"

Jake sniggered. "What the hell is a *wanker*?"

Damn. She hadn't said it to his face. Clearing her throat, she flashed him innocent eyes. "Never mind. You said something about lunch?"

Once she'd locked up and put her back in ten sign up, they headed over to the café. She felt guilty for leaving the store, but with her belly starting to rumble, she knew it was only a matter of time before she would need to make a food run anyway.

After they settled into one of the red leather booths by the window, Lily ordered her usual milkshake and fries. And ignored Jake's quirked eyebrow.

"What are you, twelve?" he joked.

"Don't judge me. We're friends now, remember? Be nice!"

He apologised through his laughter, which made the sincerity rather questionable. They went back to talking about the store. Jake had some good ideas, but they all sounded rather pricey. Apart from putting a sign out and handing out leaflets, there wasn't much else she could afford.

"I know. What about a grand opening sale?"

"But isn't today my grand opening?"

"I don't think it counts if you've not had any customers, darlin'." He flashed her a devilish smile. "How about you call today a trial and open on Saturday instead? That way we can get flyers out today and tomorrow. And people can get ten percent off if they bring the flyer in on the day. How does that sound?"

Lily sipped on her milkshake as she pondered the idea; it actually sounded like a pretty good plan. Ten percent was nothing, and it would give customers an incentive to come check the store out.

"Just one question. Don't suppose you have a printer?"

She liked this new side of Jake. Maybe they had gotten off on the wrong foot? The more they talked, the more relaxed she became. Their banter hadn't completely diminished, but she was starting to realise he wasn't the sexist twat she thought he was.

***

"No, ten percent. Ten ... percent." Lily couldn't say it any louder. "It's ... ten ... percent ... off ... *not* take it off!"

"Take it off?" Bob repeated.

Taking another deep breath, she didn't know if she even had the energy to try again. If Bob hadn't got it by now, he was never going to get it.

Just as she opened her mouth to speak again, she heard a snicker coming from behind her. Twisting around, she saw Jake slumped against the entrance of the gift shop. After shooting him her dirtiest look, which was definitely not an invitation to come closer, he sauntered over to the counter.

"It's ten percent off any item on Saturday, just bring this flyer." Jake pulled the leaflet from her clutches and handed it over to Bob.

"Ah! Ten percent! Great. I'll see you then."

Lily gawked at them both in disbelief and stuttered "how" at least three times before Jake took hold of her arm and led her out of the store.

"What the hell was that?" She found her voice on the cobblestone sidewalk.

Jake was doing a bad job of hiding his amusement. "It's your voice ... it's too high-pitched. Bob's hearing aid doesn't pick it up."

"Oh, great, so he has a sexist hearing aid!"

Letting out a frustrated groan, she began to walk away. This day, Bob and Jake could go to hell. She heard Jake shout after her but chose to ignore him. Sadly, her peace was short-lived as he soon caught up with her and blocked her path.

"Lily. Come on. It's Bob. You can't let Bob ruin your day."

"It's not just Bob. We've been doing this all afternoon and not one person has told me they would come. I thought small towns were supposed to be friendly?"

"Well, all the places I hit said they'd be there."

"Fantastic, so it's me? People hate me."

"Come on, people don't hate you." His smile grew wider as he stroked the side of her arm. "They just like me more."

Not in the mood to be teased, she pushed past him as she vocalised her sigh. This time Jake didn't follow.

Back at the store, she started to feel overwhelmed. Doubt hit her hard. Maybe she couldn't do this. Maybe all she'd ever be was someone's assistant. What did she know about running a business?

Needing a release, she turned on her speakers and closed the blinds. It was time to dance it out. Her tried-and-tested method of stress relief.

Heart pumping, eyes closed, her hips shook to the beat as she tried to silence her thoughts. The more in tune her body was to the music, the calmer she became. Songs came and went, until she finally began to feel like herself again.

A brash bang on the door eventually broke her rhythm. But that was okay. She felt better already. Catching her breath, she turned off her speakers and went to see who it was.

Jake's eyes scanned her. "Peace offering?" He held out a takeaway drinks cup. "It's a strawberry milkshake—your favourite."

Shifting aside to let him in, she accepted the drink and quickly took a big slurp.

"Y'know, I heard the music blaring from outside. Did I catch you dancing again?" His eyes twinkled as he shot her that cheeky smile.

"Maybe, why? You sad you missed the show?"

He let out a chuckle, then made himself comfortable and took a seat on top of the counter.

"Damn right I am. What's with the dancing thing? Every second you get, the music goes on."

Lily took another sip of her drink. Starting to feel her muscles ache, she shifted her body weight and leaned against one of the shelves.

"It's not a thing, I just like my music." She shrugged. "I like to dance. It relaxes me."

"Can I see?" The mischievous glint was back.

"Yeah, okay. How about you go first?" she joked.

Assuming he wouldn't take the bait, she was surprised when he quickly jumped down. Instinctively, she pushed him back on the counter, then took a seat next to him.

"Okay, all joking aside. Maybe it is a thing." She could feel his eyes on her, but she continued to concentrate on the shop floor. "I think everyone has their own way of coping with things and my way is to dance. It's something I started doing when I was a teenager, and I guess it just stuck."

"I get it. It's like a release or something?"

Lily nodded but stayed quiet.

"I chop wood. When I'm stressed. It feels really good. You ever tried?"

"Chopping wood?" She laughed. "No, you know I'm from the city, right? And I can honestly say that there has never been a need to chop any wood." She turned to face him.

"Well, I think you should try it." He beamed.

Their eyes interlocked and that's when she first felt it. Butterflies. Somersaulting in her stomach.

No. No. No. You're on a man strike, remember? And even if you weren't, you really think hooking up with your only friend's brother is a good idea?

It wasn't a good idea at all. It was a really, really stupid one.

***

As she served the last customer of the day, Lily could feel her jaw ache from a day full of smiling. All the social interaction had been exhausting. With Jake's help, the grand opening had been a success. She couldn't wait to tell him.

Locking the door, she felt her legs ache and leaned over to rub them. She couldn't remember a time when she'd worked so hard. It was certainly a change from office life.

Just as she started to make her way up to the apartment, a knock on the window forced her to turn back. Sam's excited face peered through the glass. Lily already had a hunch what this was about as she unlocked the door and let her friend inside.

"Date night!" she enthusiastically screeched, causing Lily to squint.

"It's not for two hours, Sam. I was gonna take a nice, relaxing, hot bath before we go." Her body was not going to be happy with her if she didn't at least soak her feet before forcing them into heels.

"You still can. But I'm coming upstairs too—I brought some outfits over and I need your help choosing."

Lily reluctantly agreed on the condition that she could have her bath first.

Once they were upstairs, she left Sam to freak out in the living room while Lily disappeared into the haven that was her bathroom.

As she lay in the steamy water, her stomach started to

turn. The last thing she wanted to do was go on a date. She'd only been in Bluestone for a few weeks, and she was still trying to find her bearings. Now was not the time to complicate her life with a man.

But what if the date was with Jake? You'd let him complicate your life, wouldn't you?

Suppressing her opinionated inner voice, she lay in the warm, soapy water until her legs were satisfied. Once she'd dried her hair and applied some makeup, she slipped into the only dress she'd packed. It was a simple, short crimson dress with capped sleeves. Despite how tired she was feeling, she was pleased she'd managed to make herself look half-decent.

Sam seemed to think so too as she joined her on the sofa.

"You look so pretty." Sam beamed before flapping her hands in a panic. "Okay, now you really have to help me."

Sam rose and began holding different dress options in front of her. Lily couldn't decide between two of them so she made Sam try them on.

"That's the one!" she shouted at the navy polka-dotted dress.

Lily found Sam's nerves endearing; it was now glaringly obvious just how strong her feelings for Duke were.

The restaurant where they were meeting was just a short walk from the store. Lily was pleased she didn't have to drive; she was hoping to have at least one drink to help her relax. Maybe even two, depending on how well or terrible the evening went.

Duke and Lily's date, Max, were already seated when they arrived. As Lily peered over, she knew straight away that he wasn't her type. She wasn't keen on blondes and the fact that he was skinnier than her was a major turnoff. But it didn't matter, she reminded herself. That wasn't why she was there. She was there for Sam.

Sam and Duke spent most of the night in their own conversation, leaving Lily to test out her small talk on Max. After a rocky start, things did get better once a drink was in her hand. Unfortunately, that was short-lived, as he began to get more flirtatious.

"So, you've never *been* with an American guy then?"

The question was bad enough, but when he paired it with a wink, she knew it was going to be a long night.

Fuck my life.

Sam's night on the other hand was going swimmingly, just seeing her and Duke bouncing off each other warmed Lily's heart. Everyone could see what a perfect match they were, even Max.

"The English accent is pretty sexy, bet it's even sexier in bed."

Dear Lord, give me strength.

She was beginning to get a neck ache from all the times she had to politely smile and nod. At least she knew it wasn't just awful English men that she attracted; it was awful American men too.

Her heart sank when Sam suggested that they all go to the bar next door for a drink. But seeing how happy she was, made it hard to refuse. As they left the restaurant, Lily had already started to devise an exit plan.

Desperately needing some Max-free time, she headed straight for the bathroom upon arrival and sat there a while, thinking about what excuse she could use to leave. She couldn't think of one. Not a good one anyway.

But as luck would have it, as she made her way back to the table, she spotted Jake at the bar. He had his back to her, but there was no doubt it was him. Her stomach fluttered, and before she knew it, her body was hurdling her toward him.

After placing herself next to him, she let her shoulder nudge him. "Please, for the love of God, save me."

Jake quickly turned, looking surprised to see her. "Lily? What are you doing here?"

A shiver went down her spine as he perused her outfit, paying particular attention to her bare legs. Trying her best to ignore the heat in his eyes, she choked out her reply. "I'm on the worst date ever and you have to help me." She glanced over at the table, allowing him to follow her gaze.

After looking over, he turned back to her with a face full of fury. "You're on a date with Max?" After she nodded, he continued. "And why exactly are you on a date with him?"

She didn't miss his curt tone. He was not happy.

"For your sister. She was nervous to go on a date with Duke, so I stupidly agreed to a double date."

Jake's face finally began to soften. "That bad, huh?"

"He asked me to send him a picture of my feet." She let her face say the rest and watched Jake's angry mask crack as he started to vibrate with laughter.

Lily let him get it out of his system and waited patiently for him to compose himself. Thankfully, when he was done, he agreed to help her. Although he didn't have much of a plan other than her staying with him.

"Trust me. It's a guy thing. If he thinks I'm interested, he'll back off," Jake reassured her.

With no other choice than to go along with it, he grabbed her hand and whisked her over to the dance floor.

"Oh my God, he's looking," she whispered as Jake pulled her into his arms.

"Told you. Give it a dance or two and he will get the message." Jake slowly lifted his hand and lightly pressed his fingers on the side of her cheek, gently pushing her face to mirror his. "Focus on me, not on him, or it won't work."

Being closer to him than she'd ever been, she studied his face as if for the first time. His sun-kissed skin highlighted his chiselled features and day-old stubble. But it was those eyes that caused her mouth to dry. As he watched her examine him, the hypnotising blue had even grown darker.

He pulled her closer still until not even air had a chance of surviving between their bodies. A mix of musky cologne and a scent purely Jake filled her nostrils and sent the flutters in her stomach into overdrive. Before long, his unwavering stare caused her to flush, and heat reached her cheeks. Suddenly needing an excuse to break away, she pulled back slightly and glanced over his shoulder at Max, who was still watching them.

"I told you, ignore him, darlin'." Jake's husky voice sent a tingle down her spine.

His hand took it's time travelling up her side until he reached her neckline. When he found her chin, he guided her face back to him. With their gazes locked again, she tried to silence all the thoughts running through her head. But it wasn't easy. Two more songs came and went without them taking their eyes off each other. When she finally broke the spell and looked away, she noticed Max was nowhere to be seen. Jake's plan had worked.

Self-conscious and flustered, she pulled away from his hold, unsure of where to look or how to act. "Um ... it looks like he's gone, so I think it worked."

She couldn't tell what he was thinking as he remained still. His grip on her waist didn't loosen until she took another step back. That's when she noticed something akin to disappointment overtake his face.

Was the attraction mutual or just in her head? No. It was in her head. Jake was way out of her league. He could have his pick of women.

"Good. See, I knew it would work." A flash of that confident smile made her wonder if she'd imagined the disappointment that creased his brow only a second ago.

She needed to get out of there before she embarrassed herself. "I think I'm gonna go. Leave Sam and Duke to it. Thank you for your help ... with Max." She offered up a smile and tried to scurry away. She hadn't gone far when a strong hand gripped her upper arm.

"It's late, let me walk you home." He didn't wait for her to reply, he simply placed his hand on the small of her back and led her outside.

The walk back was painful. Her nerves made her babble, but as soon as she'd detailed what happened with the shop opening, she realised she couldn't think of anything else to say. And apparently neither could Jake, so an uncomfortable silence lingered until they reached the store.

She'd definitely hit her humiliation limit for the night. After an odd half hug goodbye, she skulked up to the apartment, cursing under her breath.

CHAPTER FOUR

Only a day after her disastrous double date and Lily was really starting to question her life choices. Today's bad decision being answering the stupid phone.

"Mum, I told you, I can't talk. I'm working." Lily twiddled the pen she was holding and stared out onto the empty shop floor.

"So you've gone and bloody done it. Opened your father's shop?" Lily rolled her eyes as her mum let out another huff. "Are you trying to hurt me, Lily? Is that what you're trying to do? You know what your father leaving did to me, and now I have to deal with losing you too?"

Ever the drama queen.

"Believe it or not, Mum, not everything is about you." Lily threw the pen back onto the counter and stood.

"I just want you to come home, Lily. You don't belong there—you belong here with me and Alice."

At her wit's end, Lily didn't know what else she could possibly say and went quiet again as her mum continued.

"Sell the shop for heaven's sake and use the money to open one here, in London, if that's what you want to do. I'll even help you."

"Mum, please stop. I need to do this. If it all goes to shit,

I promise I'll come home. Just let me make my own mistakes, okay?"

The line went quiet. She could almost picture her mother's face twisting as she fought back the urge to lecture her again.

"You're more like your father than you know. Fine. Make your own mistakes, Lily. But I expect you home for your sister's birthday. Maybe I can talk some sense into you then."

"Bye, Mum." Lily hung up and slammed her phone onto the table. Needing a distraction, she walked over to the nearest shelf and began straightening the paint tins that decorated it.

Her mind started to wander back to her mother's words. She'd never compared her to Matthew before, and Lily had never even considered she might be like him. She started to rove the aisles and graze each shelf with her hand. This was all his. This is what he left her and her mum for.

Was it worth it, Dad? This shop, this life, was it worth leaving your kid for?

Before even more bitter questions could fill her head, the door creaked open. She abruptly turned to see Sam's smiling face and mud-caked denims.

"Let me guess, you and Duke took a roll in the hay?" Lily laughed.

"Ha. Ha. Where did you run off to last night?" Sam made a beeline for the seat behind the counter. "You fall down the toilet?"

Avoiding eye contact, Lily went back to fiddling with the paint tins. "I'm sorry, I actually ran into your brother and we got chatting."

"So ... you and Jake?" Sam's gaze penetrated into the side of Lily's head; she could tell her eyebrows would be raised even before she snuck a peek at her friend.

"Yeah." She hoped Sam didn't notice the rush of blood filling her cheeks. "We were just catching up about the launch and stuff. When I looked over at you guys, I noticed

Max had left, so I called it a night too, left the lovebirds to it."

"I'm not gonna let you tease me; I'm in too good a mood." Sam couldn't wipe the smile off her face. "We kissed. Duke and I kissed."

"What? No way! Okay, you need to tell me everything."

As she listened to Sam gush about Duke, Lily couldn't help but think back to Jake. Just remembering being in his arms made her feel things she hadn't felt in a while.

Oh God, why does he have to be so damn hot?

Trying hard to banish her thoughts, her focus returned to Sam.

"So, you'll come over tomorrow? And help me?"

Fuck. What is she talking about?

"Um, yes, of course. I'll be there—what time again?"

Having unknowingly offered up her services, Lily just hoped Jake wasn't around tomorrow.

***

After her fourth pep talk in the bathroom mirror, Lily eventually dragged herself away and back to the dining table. She thought she'd agreed to help dress Sam for her date, not participate in it. Again.

Jake attempted to smile at her as she took her seat back at the table, but she had yet to meet his gaze. They still hadn't spoken without the aid of Sam or Duke, and things were growing more uncomfortable by the minute.

The tasty meal Sam had whipped up was the only saving grace of the evening. Eating also gave Lily the perfect excuse not to engage in conversation. Unfortunately, once she'd cleared her plate, she went back to not knowing where to look or what to say.

"I've got something I wanna show you," Jake whispered as he leaned over the table. "Wanna get out of here?"

She wanted to leave so badly but was well aware that if she didn't know what to say to Jake now, it would be even harder once they were alone.

Sensing her hesitation, he tried again. "It will be worth it, I promise."

As he flashed his teeth, all those feelings she was trying to suppress came rushing back.

After reluctantly agreeing, they excused themselves and left Sam and Duke alone.

As soon as they left the house, Jake grabbed her hand and led her to the bottom of the garden. It wasn't until they walked farther through a cluster of trees that reflected the last of the sunlight that she realised how late it was.

"Where are you taking me?"

What a great idea, Lily. Follow the hot man into an abandoned field … in the dark. You just better bloody hope he's not a serial killer.

Jake stopped and turned back to look at her. "I told you, there's something I want to show you."

Yep, that sounds like something a killer would say. You're dead. Should've listened to your head and not your hormones.

He went back to tugging her hand as she followed behind him until they were further into the trees. After a few more minutes, he finally came to a halt. Lily's eyes were firmly on Jake as she stood next to him. He was in front of an old wooden bench and staring into the darkness. Once she was satisfied that he wasn't about to pull out a knife, she followed his gaze, only to discover a riverbed just two hundred yards away.

"Wow, now that's a view." She gawked as her eyes followed the ripples that danced across the stream.

Eyes transfixed, she breathed in the fresh air and let the last of the heat from the deep orange light absorb into her skin. This is why she'd come here. This was something she couldn't get back home. Peace.

"Pretty cool, huh?"

She glimpsed over at him, expecting to see that cocky grin, but he appeared almost humble. As if he was just as in awe of their surroundings as she was. She watched as he slowly took a seat on the bench and then decided to join him.

"When chopping wood doesn't work, I come here," he announced.

They both sat quietly for a while, but this time it was in a comfortable silence. A peaceful one.

As it continued to grow darker and darker, Lily found the courage to ask him about Matthew.

"Can I ask you something?" She fiddled with the sleeve of her hoodie until he agreed. "You were close to my dad, right?"

"Sure. He was a friend."

"What was he like?" She looked back up, just in time to see his expression flick from curiosity to sympathy.

Jake cleared his throat. "Um, he was a good guy. Quiet. Liked to keep himself to himself, but he had a good heart."

The metallic taste of blood filled her mouth as she bit down on her lip. She felt pathetic. Having to ask a complete stranger to tell her more about her own father. But she wanted to know. Especially after the snarky comment her mother had made yesterday. Lily wanted to know if she was like him.

"How did you know ... that he had a good heart?"

Jake took a deep breath and looked down at his boots. "When my dad"—he paused—"when I lost my dad, Matt was there. He came by every day for a year. He always had some excuse. Like bringing over mail or food, or pretending he wanted us to test out some new product. But I knew why he was coming. He wanted to make sure we were okay."

She went silent for a moment and turned her attention back to the water. After eventually letting go of her clasped bottom lip, she spoke again. "You know, I was five when he left. I never heard from him or saw him after that. I'm glad to hear there was some goodness there, but it also makes me wonder why he could be there for you guys but not for his own daughter."

Jake freed one of her hands from under her sleeve and laced his fingers through hers. "I'm sorry, Lily. I didn't know. I wish I had more answers for you."

"It's okay. You don't have anything to be sorry for." She looked down at their intertwined hands. "I guess, coming here, I thought maybe I would understand him more. Why he did what he did. It's stupid, I know."

"It's not stupid. Not at all, Lily." He twisted his body to face her and used his free hand to lightly turn her cheek to face him. "Let me help you. I'll try my hardest to answer any questions you have, and if I don't know, then I'll help you find someone who does."

She appreciated the sentiment, even if it was only because he felt sorry for her.

"Thank you. Why are you being so nice to me?"

"Maybe I've got a thing for women who curse like truckers."

She let out a chuckle while Jake pulled out his phone with his left hand and started fumbling with it. The next thing she knew, country music started to blare out of it. After placing it on the bench, he rose and pulled her up with him, using the hand he still clung to.

"Dance it out?"

Lily vigorously shook her head. But Jake wasn't giving up. He readjusted their position until his hands were on her waist and her arms were flung around his neck.

"So, what, you're gonna sway me into submission?" She smirked as he began to move them to the rhythm.

"If that's what it takes, darlin'."

Any courage she'd mustered quickly dispersed as she stared back into those deep blue eyes.

Fuck.

She gulped as his gaze didn't waver. Every time she attempted to look away, his finger grazed her cheek to bring her right back to him. It got so intense she was relieved when a faster song came on.

Encouraging him to pick up the pace, swaying turned to spinning. Unfortunately, after only a few spins, she found herself the victim of an overenthusiastic twirl. Stumbling over his foot, she quickly lost her balance. Thankfully, instead of face planting into the dirt, Jake caught her fall and managed to keep her steady by tightening his hold on her waist.

Lily found herself gazing into those darkening eyes once again, and her heart started to hammer. As Jake tightened his grip, she felt goosebumps break out on the exposed skin under where his hands lay. Despite the hem of her top riding up, her skin was almost burning from his touch. But she couldn't move; she felt frozen, even her eyes on his were locked in place.

His head dipped and his face got closer. Her breath now shallow, she watched on like a spectator as he closed the gap between them. But as soon as his warm breath hit her lips, she jerked and abruptly pulled free of his hold.

Fuck, fuck, fuck, fuck, fuck.

She had to turn her head, if she looked into those eyes again, she knew there would be no going back. Once she'd managed to mumble an excuse about it getting late, she hastily made her way back to the house without turning back.

***

The next day, Lily sat cross-legged on her living room floor with paper scattered around her. In an attempt to stop herself from thinking about Jake, she'd decided to throw herself into finding answers. She'd hoped that there might be some hidden in the boxes, but so far she was yet to find them. She reached over for her drink, then took another gulp before letting out a heavy sigh.

As she mentally prepared herself to open the next box, her phone started to ring. Scrambling to find it, she flung papers up in the air until she finally discovered it under one of the many pictures she'd come across.

It was her sister, Alice. "Hey, Ali, how you doing?"

"I miss you, Lilypad. Y'know Mum is losing her shit,

right?"

Lily's lips twitched. "When is she not losing her shit? Don't tell me—she's asked you to call me and convince me to come home?"

"Well, yes. But that's not why I'm calling. I just wanted to see if you're okay?"

Lily looked around at the boxes surrounding her. "I opened his shop. I now sell drills, nails and barbed wire to the good people of Bluestone County."

"Wow, you really did it?"

"Yep, I'm not coming back, Ali."

She could hear Alice sighing down the line. "Look, Lily, being there won't bring him back. It won't give you the answers you've been looking for."

"You think I'm here to find out why he left?" She stared at the picture of Matthew laying on the pile in front of her.

"Yeah. I do. And I think you're gonna be disappointed when you realise that you will never know."

"You have a dad, Ali, a real dad. I have a stepdad and a dead biological father who left and never said why. If you were me, wouldn't you want answers?"

"So, you are there for answers?"

Lily went quiet for a moment; Alice would never understand. "Maybe, but that's not the only reason. You know I wasn't happy back home; I needed a change, a fresh start."

It wasn't just her depressing job she didn't miss; it was everything. Her tiny shoebox-sized flat, which was too hot in the summer and freezing cold in the winter, was up there. Then there was the smoggy air that clogged up her pores and left black stains on her makeup wipes. And let's not forget about her mother; there really was something comforting about being a nine-hour flight away from her. Lily felt free. Finally.

"I know, Lily, I just wish your fresh start wasn't so far away. You're my sister and I love you. It's only been a month and I miss you like crazy."

"Me too, Ali. Me too."

She supposed that was the only downside. Not having Alice around. If only Lily could transport Alice here. Then everything would be perfect.

CHAPTER FIVE

The hot sun blazed down on Jake as he climbed back onto his horse and headed home. It was early afternoon, and all the guests were finally happy and occupied.

After wiping sweat from his brow, he carefully dismounted and led Rocky back to his stable. On his way back to the house, Lily flashed through his mind again. He still couldn't figure her out. Why did she keep running away from him? First the bar and then during their dance. Every time he thought they were going to kiss, she took off faster than a speeding bullet. Their attraction wasn't in his head. He'd felt it. The way she looked at him and the way she blushed when he touched her … it was obvious something was there. She wanted to kiss him just as much as he wanted to kiss her. So the running just didn't make any sense.

"Damn, you stink!" Sam yelled as he entered the kitchen.

Jake let out a snigger. "Nice to see you too, sis." He began searching the fridge for something to quench his thirst. "Aren't you supposed to be giving riding lessons?"

"I'm done for the day; my last lesson cancelled," she announced. "I was actually gonna stop by the store and give Lily a hand for a bit."

His ears pricked up at that. He hadn't gotten the chance

to talk to her since she'd run away from him. The one time he dropped by the store to see her, she had to excuse herself to make a fake phone call. Taking a swig of his juice, he rested against the countertop. "Is the store busy? Cos I can come help too?"

He noticed Sam's eyebrow raise and instantly regretted his offer.

"You wanna help?" Clicking her tongue, she continued. "You and Lily seemed to have put your differences aside, haven't you?"

"Yeah, she doesn't wanna kick me in the balls anymore, if that's what you mean." Attempting to mask his discomfort, he took another drink of juice.

"You never did tell me where you guys wandered off to the other night?"

"Well, it was pretty clear that you and Duke wanted to be alone, so we made ourselves scarce."

He watched as Sam hummed to herself for a moment. "We're gonna head to Mickey's after closing—you should come meet us there."

He agreed, trying hard not to look too pleased with the invite.

It wasn't perfect. He wouldn't be able to talk to her properly while Sam was there and watching him. Especially now that she was suspicious. It was hard to keep anything from his sister. But being able to see and spend time with Lily was enough to put a big smile on his face.

As he contemplated how he was going to get her alone, the smell of sweat and horse reached his nose. Sam was right; he did stink. Time for a shower. He didn't want to give Lily another reason to run from him.

***

Lily and Sam were already at the bar when he arrived. Starting to feel nervous, he tried to recall the last time a girl had made him feel this way.

No one has even come close. That's why you can't stop thinking about her.

With daylight still in sight, the normal Friday night crowd was yet to descend on Mickey's. Jake hardly recognised his old haunt in the cold light of day as he made his way past the empty, chipped wood tables. The ancient jukebox rattled out a familiar tune, while he could almost taste the stench of stale beer that filled the room.

Taking a seat at their table, he immediately noticed the shock on Lily's face. After a stilted greeting, he scanned her for clues as to how she was feeling. Met with just a shy pout, she was hesitant to maintain eye contact. His presence had evidently once again brought out the more timid side of her.

Sam, unhelpfully, hadn't informed Lily that he was going to be joining them and conversation wasn't flowing quite so easily. A drink run to the bar gave him a welcome relief and the chance to regroup.

"Hey, Teddy, whiskey straight up and whatever the ladies are having." He waved in the direction of Sam and Lily and pressed himself against the bar.

"Sure thing," Teddy replied as he lined up the glasses. "You asked her out yet?"

"What?"

"The new girl, Lily. You asked her out yet? I saw you guys dancing together the other night. You looked pretty cosy." He grinned as he squirted Coke into one of the drinks.

"I don't know what you're talking about, Teddy—we're just friends."

"Yeah, yeah." Teddy chuckled as he passed over the drinks. "Whatever you say, Jake. Just trying to keep up on town gossip, that's all. There's been a lotta guys asking about her, so I'll just tell 'em she's single."

Like hell you will.

"And let them harass her until she agrees to a date, I don't think so. Tell them she's taken."

Ignoring Teddy's smug grin, Jake settled up and took his

first swig of whiskey. Right. He was ready to try again.

Lily stroked back a long strand of her golden hair and allowed her lips to tip up as he passed her over the glass. Giving him a smile that lit up her whole face. The higher her cheeks raised, the more her emerald eyes sparkled.

"Actually, Jake, you might be able to help me." His attention was piqued. "I don't suppose you know anything about the person who owned the store before my dad? Only I found some old contracts, and it looks as though my dad inherited the store too."

Shifting in his seat, he tried to think back to before Matt had come to town. Only a kid at that time, his memory couldn't be trusted.

"Um, I'm not sure I can remember, but I know how we could find out." It was perfect, a way to help and an excuse to spend more time with her. "We should go to the local library. Stan, who works there, will know. I can take you there tomorrow?"

"That's generous of you," Sam piped, her distrustful glare on him. "Don't you have that riding tour tomorrow?"

Jake cleared his throat. "Yeah, I do, but I should be done by lunchtime." He turned back to Lily. "I can pick you up at one? It shouldn't take too long."

Before Sam could say anything, Lily beamed back over at him and placed her hand on his arm. "That would be amazing. Thank you. If you're sure you don't mind?"

"No problem at all." He felt his smile widen as he looked back into her eyes. It was then he knew that he would do anything she asked.

Conversation got easier after that, and they started talking about the ranch. Lily had a million questions and was keen to find out more about the activities they offered. He was happy to answer all of her questions and then some, but he couldn't help but notice Sam's eyes on him.

Just as he was explaining how trail horses were chosen, Lily's ringtone blasted out and stopped him mid-sentence. After fumbling in her purse for a moment, she pulled out the device and stared down at the screen. Immediately apologising, she then went on to excuse herself. Leaving Jake alone with Sam.

"What are you doing?" Sam chirped as soon as Lily was out of earshot.

"What?"

"Are you hitting on her?" Sam was unimpressed.

"No, I'm not hitting on her." His denial wasn't even convincing himself.

"Don't lie to me, Jake. I'm your sister. I know when you're lying. You like her, don't you?"

A heavy sigh slipped out. "I ... um, I don't know. Maybe." He paused before giving in. "So what if I do?"

Once his sister was done cursing a blue streak, she turned to him. Disappointment clear on her face. "She's my friend, Jake. Not one of your bimbos. I'm not gonna let you hurt her."

Knowing Sam wasn't going to go easy on him, he took another healthy gulp of his drink. It was fair to say he didn't have the best reputation with women, but that didn't mean it didn't sting when his own sister automatically assumed the worst.

"And that's what you think I'll do, hurt her? You really have that little faith in me?"

"She's vulnerable, Jake. She's just lost her dad and moved halfway across the world to start a new life. Trust me, if you really like her, then you'll back off."

Backing off was the last thing he wanted to do. But hurting Lily wasn't an option either. Torn, he decided to seek Sam's advice. "Okay, I'm listening. *If* I wait ... how long would I be waiting for?"

"Well, if you *insist* on making a move on her, then just give her a few months to settle in at least."

"A few months!" Lily was all he'd been thinking about since she'd swayed those sexy hips into town. He could barely wait a day to see her let alone months.

"I'm serious, Jake. If you genuinely like her, then you will still like her a few months from now. And if that's the case, then you'll have my blessing. I'll even put in a good word."

He didn't want to wait, but he didn't want the wrath of his sister either. After eventually agreeing to think about it, he suddenly had the urge for another drink. It was time to pay Teddy another visit at the bar.

***

The old library still had the same eery silence that unnerved him as a kid. Even the smell was familiar, the sweet, musky scent had hit him as soon as he'd walked through the doors and still lingered on the tip of his nose.

Jake and Lily sat amongst the books, with rows of bookshelves towering over them. As they continued to watch Stan rummage through his stack of papers, Jake glanced over at Lily once again. She was wearing her fitted jeans and a black camisole with a lacy neckline. He'd had to stop himself from drooling when he picked her up. Even in something so casual, she was the most beautiful woman he'd ever seen. How could he wait months to ask her out when he was struggling to even make it through today?

"Ah ha!" Stan bellowed as he lifted the paper he had been holding. "This is it. A Mr. T. A. Barnes."

"So, Mr. Barnes owned the store before Matthew?" Lily eagerly leaned forward.

"Yes. It looks like Mr. Barnes left it to Matthew in his will," Stan replied.

"Don't suppose there are any clues there as to why he did that?" Jake asked as he looked back at Lily, who had started to bite down on her lip.

Stan scrutinised the document again, pushing his glasses back up. "It doesn't say here, but I can obtain a copy of the will for you, if you'd like? Maybe that might tell you."

"You can do that? Yes, yes, please, that would be amazing. Thank you." Lily's face lit up with excitement.

"The court clerk's office should have it on file, just give

me a day or two." Stan smiled warmly at them both.

"Thank you, Stan. Thank you so much." He felt a twinge as he caught another glimpse of Lily's happy face.

Once they'd left the library, Jake convinced her to grab some food with him. The pastry shop on the corner had the best peach pie around and he was keen to impress her with it.

Yes, because pie will make her like you.

"You think knowing will give you some answers?"

Lily took another sip of her coffee and let the mug warm her hands. "I don't know. Maybe. I guess I've just never known why he came down here. Of all the places in the world, y'know, why here, why Bluestone?"

It was indeed a mystery. He was still getting his head around it all. In all the years he'd known Matt, he never struck him as the kind of man who could just walk away from his family.

"Whatever the reason though. It doesn't change the fact that he left." Jake contemplated, trying his best not to think about his own mother and her sudden departure.

She let out a small sigh as she placed her mug back onto the delicate white table. "Yeah. I guess, knowing won't change the past, but it might give me some peace."

As her eyes became misty, he wished there were something more he could do for her.

"Why did you come here, really?"

"Haven't we already had this conversation?" A small smile started to tilt up.

"You know that a vague answer doesn't count as a conversation, right?"

The waitress placed their plates on the table, interrupting their conversation, causing a heavenly waft of peach pie to hit the back of his throat.

"I wasn't happy back home. I hated my shitty job, my tiny flat, my disastrous love life. There wasn't anything keeping me there. So, when I found out about this place, I don't know … it kinda felt like fate, like this was an opportunity for me to start again someplace new." Lily turned her attention to the pie.

"Disastrous love life? I thought all English guys were handsome and charming?"

She scoffed. "Well, I don't know where those English guys live, but it's definitely not London."

Never one to miss an opportunity, Jake prodded for more. "So what kind of guy are you looking for?"

"Well, handsome and charming sound like a good start." She giggled as she took her first bite.

He tried not to laugh at her moans as she devoured the pie. Instead, he used the distraction to find out more about what she was looking for in a man.

"But if you had to list their attributes?"

"There is no list. I'm thirty-two; I'm well aware that the perfect man doesn't exist. To be honest, I kinda know what I don't want more than what I do want. If that makes sense?"

"I'm listening."

"Okay. Well, I guess no one who cheats or lies and takes my trust for granted. And no one selfish or mean. I want someone with a good heart."

"So basically, no heartless, cheating liars then?"

They both started to laugh, and he could swear she actually glowed.

"Seriously, though, you laugh, but you've basically just described every guy I've ever dated."

"For real?"

"Yep."

What the hell was wrong with those men? Who would be stupid enough to cheat on this woman or let her go?

"Okay. Looks wise … what do you go for?"

Please say tall, dark with blue eyes.

"Nope"—Lily shook her head—"it's your turn. What do you go for?"

He considered his words for a moment, but then thought, screw it.

"Okay, darlin', but then it's your turn." After a wink, he leaned back in his chair and made sure her eyes were locked on his. "Long, wavy blonde hair, green eyes and an English accent." As he watched her cheeks turn a deep shade of pink, he couldn't help but grin. There was no going back now.

Or so he thought. That was about the time that Lily decided to run again.

"Umm … I need to get back to the store."

Before he could reply, she'd tossed money onto the table and scampered out the door.

Shit.

CHAPTER SIX

"What the hell are you doing here?" Lily shrieked in excitement.

Alice stood grinning in the store entrance, suitcase in tow. She was in one of her bright, floral dresses with her dark hair tied into a messy bun.

"Well, you invited me to come visit. So, I'm visiting!"

Lily jumped into her arms. If ever she needed her sister, it was now. "Why didn't you say anything? I could have picked you up from the airport!"

"Don't be silly—I got a taxi. You really are in the arse-end of nowhere, aren't you?" Alice wheeled her suitcase in and looked around at the store. "So, this is it. This is the famous hardware store he left you."

Lily started to feel tense while her eyes assessed the shop floor. "Yep. This is it. Come on, let's go upstairs; I'll show you the flat he left me too."

Once they were upstairs, she started to feel guilty that she'd neglected the apartment. Getting the store open was her main priority, which is why the space still looked as depressing as the day she'd arrived. The majority of Matthew's things were still bagged up and lined the hallway and were the first thing Alice noticed as she began snooping.

Within minutes she'd dug out an old picture from one of the bags.

"This him?"

"I'm gonna need a drink before we start opening those." Lily headed straight for the kitchen and grabbed them a bottle of wine.

As they cosied up on the sofa, she wanted answers.

"Okay, Ali, spill. What's with all the secrecy? Why didn't you tell me you were coming, and how did you get the time off?"

"I missed you, Lilypad." She shrugged. "Plus, Mum is driving me absolutely crazy. And I had loadsa holiday saved up, so I just thought I'd come see you."

"Did Mum send you here? Be honest."

Alice let out a chuckle. "She didn't send me here, I promise. I just missed you. Y'know this is the longest we've gone without seeing each other?"

Relieved her sister wasn't on a covert mission to bring her home, Lily started to relax. She filled Alice in on the details of her stay so far. She might have mentioned Jake too but purposefully left out the embarrassing crush part. Then she remembered the news she got earlier today from Stan.

"It turns out, he inherited this place from his biological father. I didn't even know he was adopted."

"Damn, look at you. Detective Lily!" Alice teased. "It's weird, I get it. But just because his biological dad left him this place, didn't mean he had to up and leave you and Mum. I don't understand what exactly it is you're looking for."

Lily stared into her glass. She knew Alice was right, knowing why he came here didn't change anything. He still left.

"So, when do I get to meet this Jake guy?" Alice threw her a mischievous look.

"He's just a friend, and you'll get to meet him tomorrow. We're going to a barbecue at the ranch."

"A friend my arse. You're practically blushing at the

mention of his name."

Seriously? What the hell? Stupid, traitorous red face.

"No, I'm not!" Lily protested as she grabbed a cushion and pelted Alice with it.

***

"You're not wearing that," Alice chimed as Lily grabbed her keys.

"What do you mean? What's wrong with it?" She scanned her outfit in confusion.

"You're gonna see the lovely Jake in jeans and a T-shirt?" Alice pointed disapprovingly at her.

"For the millionth time, he's just a——" Before she could finish, Alice cut her off.

"Just a friend. I know, I know." She grabbed Lily's hand and led her back into the bedroom. "Friend or no friend, you're not wearing that."

After rummaging through her wardrobe, Alice pulled out her denim shorts and a lacy camisole and threw them onto the bed. "Here you go. Perfect."

Lily wasn't impressed. "I'll freeze, are you insane?"

"Are you kidding? It's so hot here compared to back home. Just put it on and we'll shove a cardigan in the car, yeah?"

Reluctantly getting changed, Lily already knew there wasn't much point in fighting her sister. As the youngest, Alice was used to getting her way.

Lily used the drive as an excuse to show Alice some of the scenery Bluestone County had to offer. Staying in the centre of town was deceiving—outside of it, there were miles and miles of picturesque farms, fields and rolling hills. It also killed some time. She wasn't looking forward to seeing Jake again after running out on him a second time.

As they pulled up to the ranch, the beauty of it still took her back, even Alice was captivated. The fresh air blew through their hair and down into their lungs as they got out of the car. But before they made their way round to the back, Lily froze.

Feeling self-conscious, she grabbed her cardigan from the backseat and wrapped it around her. Much to Alice's dismay.

A few tuts later, they followed the smoky aroma.

She was excited to introduce her sister to Sam, who immediately came running over to meet them. As Lily introduced them, she caught sight of Jake. Ignoring the butterflies that were taking flight in her stomach, she returned his wave.

Please don't come over. Please don't come over.

Her chant didn't work. As soon as they each took a seat around the fire, Jake was on his way over to them.

Shit. Be cool. Don't say something stupid.

"Ladies." He politely tipped his head to greet them. After which, his eyes quickly darted back to her and up and down her outfit. "You look nice tonight, Lily."

Fiddling with the sleeves of her cardigan, she thanked him with a nervous smile.

While Alice introduced herself, Lily gave herself an internal pep talk. She was finding it hard to even look Jake in the eye. Luckily for her, her sister was a social butterfly and could fill any silence. It gave her a chance to just sit back for a while and organise her thoughts.

Ignoring her discomfort, Jake suggested they go gather some food for everyone. Food was a welcome distraction, being alone with Jake, however, was not. But he knew she wasn't going to flat out say no in front of Sam and Alice, so she begrudgingly followed him.

"Your sister seems nice," he said as he filled the plate she was holding with burgers.

"Yeah, it's really good to see her."

"You okay? You're quieter than usual tonight."

Um, no, I'm not okay. Is he seriously going to pretend that I didn't run out on him the other day like a lunatic?

Apparently, he was. Which led to her blaming her mood

and awkwardness on Matthew. After all, her trauma might as well be useful for once. "Stan came by yesterday. Turns out my dad inherited the place from his biological father."

"Matt was adopted?" Jake's eyebrow quirked up.

"Yep, apparently so." Grabbing another plate for him to fill, she placed the other one down. "I'm sorry, I'm just a bit distracted, what with that and Alice showing up unannounced."

"Sounds like you need a break." Lily could almost see the lightbulb switch on in his head. "Come on, let's go get some drinks before we take this over."

Taking the plate from her, he replaced it with his hand and led her into the house. His grip was strong but gentle and made her damn knees weak again. She felt her heart pump faster as he led her into the living room and sat her on the sofa.

Disappearing for a moment, he soon returned with drinks and passed her over a glass of wine.

"We can hide out here until you feel better." He joined her on the couch.

She let out a nervous laugh. "I really looked that desperate?"

His smile widened. "No, you look really beautiful." Feeling flush, she knew it wouldn't be long before her cheeks began to redden. "But you also look a little overwhelmed. I'm guessing that's cos of what you found out about your dad?"

Nope. That'll be you calling me beautiful.

She was suddenly glad she was holding a large glass of wine; she took a big gulp before continuing the only conversation topic that would be safe right now. "Alice doesn't get it. Why I'm here, why I'm still looking for an answer to an inexcusable decision."

"But she has a dad, right, your stepdad?" He waited for her to nod before carrying on. "She's not gonna get it. But that's okay, she doesn't have to. You're here for you, no one else."

How did he do that, she wondered. How did he manage to always say the right thing and make her feel better?

"Yeah. You're right. When did you get so wise?" she asked, playfully poking him.

"Don't act all surprised. I'm more than just a pretty face, sweetheart. I'm the full package, brawn and brains." He laughed.

"I'm so sorry," she replied sarcastically, "I didn't mean to objectify you, Jake. You are, of course, more than just *sort of* hard abs."

She began to giggle as he pretended to take offence and forced her hand onto his chest. "Don't you mean rock-hard abs! See?" he cried.

As he pushed her hand down again, he yanked her into him. All of a sudden it wasn't just laughter coursing through her, but a whole hell load of electricity too. An all too familiar tension filled the air as their amusement began to wane. This was usually the time when she would freak out and pull away, but this time she remained still, curiosity getting the best of her.

Her gaze flicked from his eyes to his lips, which were slowly moving closer to hers. Her heart pounded in anticipation, the nearer he got, the more lightheaded she became. Then, to her surprise, he pulled back. Well, more like jolted before abruptly standing.

"Um, Sam is probably ..." he spluttered. "Sam and Alice are probably wondering where we are. I should ... I should go grab them their food."

Before she had a chance to reply, he had already gone.

What the actual fuck?

She sat quietly in disbelief. Was she going crazy? There had been signs, right?

Shit. Is it all in my head? The attraction is just one way. Could it be that he's just a flirtatious person and I've read it all wrong?

Overcome with embarrassment, she couldn't face going out there just yet. It took another ten minutes and another glass of wine before she eventually ventured out again.

Sam and Alice were yapping away as Lily took a seat with them. Thankfully, they didn't ask any questions and offered up some food instead.

"Alice and I have agreed that Saturday night is girls' night. You and Alice are gonna spend the night here, and we're gonna watch trashy movies and eat loadsa junk— doesn't that sound fun?" Sam said excitedly.

"Yeah, sounds fun." Lily tried her hardest to match their enthusiasm.

She was glad they were getting on. She was suddenly not in the most sociable mood, so she let Alice take the lead while she spent the rest of the night avoiding Jake, which was actually easier than she thought because he was avoiding her too.

***

"Okay, spill it. What happened?" Alice asked as they got ready for bed.

"What? I don't know what you're talking about."

"You're the worst liar ever! I'm not stupid, y'know? You and Jake disappeared for a bit, and then you re-emerged with a face like a slapped arse. Now, are you gonna tell me what happened, or continue to pout for the rest of the night?"

It had always been hard to keep anything a secret from Alice. She knew her inside out. It was infuriating.

"Fine." Lily slumped onto the bed. "We went inside for a drink and almost kissed. Again."

"Again? Okay, back up. I have two questions: when did you almost kiss before and why didn't you kiss this time?" Alice jumped on the bed too.

"It really doesn't matter, because it's pretty clear after tonight that he's not into me like that anyway." Lily pulled at her pyjama shorts, too embarrassed to catch her sister's gaze.

"What makes you think that?"

"He pulled away. You should've seen him; he couldn't get out of there quick enough." Lily sulkily replied.

"Wait a minute, so you almost kiss again, and he runs away? What happened the other times you almost kissed?"

Lily went on to explain about the moments they had at the bar, at the ranch and the comments he'd made at the coffee shop. After tonight, she was questioning everything, so it actually felt good to let it all out. God knows she could do with a second opinion.

"Listen, Lily, guys don't say or do shit like that unless they're interested. Now, I don't know what happened in that room, but I did see the way that man was looking at you. And let me tell you something, Lilypad, the dude's got it bad."

Lily wanted to believe her, but the evidence was right there. "Trust me, you wouldn't be saying that if you'd witnessed how quickly he fled."

She knew Alice's instincts were to analyse and discuss for hours on end, so she decided to stop her in her tracks. "It's for the best, Ali. The last thing I need right now is to be distracted."

***

It was girl's night at the ranch, and just one movie in, Lily was already tired. The seven-day weeks had finally caught up to her, and every muscle in her body was rebelling.

"Lily, if you fall asleep at nine o'clock, I'm officially disowning you!" Alice screeched over at her.

Pulling herself up, she reached for another slice of pizza. If anything could keep her awake, it was cheese.

The subject soon veered from the movie to men. Sam gushed about Duke, while Alice relayed cute stories about her boyfriend, Rob. With nothing to contribute herself, not even the cheese was lifting her mood.

Lily had no other choice but to drink her sorrows away.

Already three drinks into the night, she stumbled over to the kitchen in search of more. It wasn't until she'd been staring into the fridge for a good few minutes that she realised she was a tiny bit tipsy.

Finally spotting a bottle of wine, she grabbed it and spun around to find Jake grinning at her.

"You're drunk." His eyes roved over her.

"What? No, I'm not," she replied while trying to straighten herself up.

"Yes, you are, darlin'." He was obviously finding it all very amusing. "Wow, so this is what drunk Lily looks like?"

"Whatever. I need more wine, so if you'll excuse me, I need to go drink this." She could hear herself slur as she held the bottle out in front of her.

Through Jake's laughs, he took the bottle from her and guided her onto one of the breakfast stools. "How about I get you a glass of water first? And then you can have your wine."

"Why do you even care?" She let herself droop over the counter as she watched him pour her a glass of water. "You don't even like me."

"What? What are you talking about?"

The clank of the glass hitting the surface caused her head to twitch. "You know what I'm talking about."

Taking a seat next to her, he tried to get her to take a sip of the water. Gently pushing the hair out of her face, his features were soft and full of concern. "Of course I like you, Lily. Here, drink this, it will make you feel better."

She succumbed and took a sip. "Then why did you run away?" As soon as she said it, she wished she could take it back.

"You think"—Jake stopped and took a deep breath—"you think I don't like you?" His eyes burnt into her. "I didn't run away. I mean, I did, but not because of that."

Straightening up, she stayed quiet but maintained eye contact. There was something hidden in his stare, and she wanted to find out what.

"I promised Sam that I wouldn't—um."

"You find the wine?" Alice bellowed as she stumbled into the kitchen.

Unaware of the conversation she'd just broken up, she cheerily grabbed the bottle and tugged at Lily's sleeve. "Come on, Lily, no boys allowed on girls' night! Sorry, Jake, we're gonna have to love you and leave you."

Back in the living room, Jake's words niggled her. He'd promised Sam. What did that mean? Had she told him to stay away from her? Or was it just the start of some excuse that would allow him to let her down gently?

As the second movie played, she pondered asking Sam. But each time Lily tried, she ended up chickening out. Instead, she comforted herself with more wine and crisps until she eventually passed out.

CHAPTER SEVEN

It was the second week of Alice's visit, and she'd settled into Bluestone life with ease. Lily tried hard not to think about her looming leaving date and instead focused on the positives of having her sister around.

Not only had Alice covered for Lily at the store so she could get some much-needed rest, but she'd also helped find her a weekend shop assistant. The thought of having weekends off again was exciting.

As they closed up for the night, they discussed their dinner plans. Lily's stomach was already rumbling, but she knew she couldn't subject Alice to another night of her cooking.

"We can go to the café, or Mickey's?" Her suggestions were both within walking distance; she wasn't in the mood to drive anywhere.

"Let's do the café—those chips are pretty drool-worthy," Alice said as she changed the door sign to closed.

After a quick change, they headed out. The café was just across the street, and because it was still early, it was really quiet.

With just two other diners, they had their pick of seats. Alice quickly slid into one of the booths by the window and started scanning the menu.

They ordered straight away, eager to satisfy their cravings.

"I don't want you to leave." Lily curled her lips. "Can't you stay longer?"

Alice placed her hand on top of hers. "I wish I could, Lilypad." She glanced out the window and then back at her. "I can see why you like it here, y'know? It's got that quiet, tranquil vibe going on. Nothing like back home."

"It's what I needed." Lily paused for a moment. "I didn't realise how unhappy I was back home until I came here."

Alice's grip on her hand tightened. "I feel bad that I didn't know. Why didn't you tell me?"

Their hands broke apart as the waitress placed down their drinks.

"I don't think I realised myself. Not until I found out about Matthew and the store." She shuddered as she thought back to her old assistant job and the grey cubicle that imprisoned her. "It's like I'd been living the same day over and over again, only nothing ever happened. I was trapped in my own boring version of fucking Groundhog Day."

Alice giggled. "No offence, but Bluestone isn't exactly the liveliest of places to run away to."

"I know, I know. But I'm not here to do the things I can do back home. Coming here … it was about taking a chance … a risk." Lily was finding it difficult to explain. "I'm sick of the city. I'm sick of spending eight hours a day in an airless office filled with narcissists and psychopaths. I want something else. Something more."

Hoping she would understand, she watched as the lines on Alice's forehead started to crinkle. "And this is the life you want? A small town in the middle of nowhere?"

"Believe it or not, yeah, this is what I want." Lily gestured out the window. "It's beautiful here, Ali, and I have things here that I could never have back home. Fresh air, long walks, my own business … the list goes on."

She could tell Alice was struggling. Instead of forcing her to understand, she decided to end it there and changed the subject.

In between slurping on their milkshakes and stuffing themselves with fries, they caught up on gossip. She learned more about Rob's recent promotion at the marketing agency; Steve, her stepdad, and his new obsession with archery and Mum's latest fixation on when and where Alice and Rob would be getting married.

As much as her mother drove her crazy, she had to admit that a part of Lily missed her. A very small part. It didn't help that their once friendly weekly coffee dates had now turned into weekly guilt trips over the phone, making it hard to talk about anything other than her total abandonment.

With her belly full, Lily sank back into the chair and gazed out of the window.

"You looking for loverboy?" Alice teased.

It seemed about right; Lily hadn't heard a Jake joke in hours. She refused to rise to it and just shot her a look.

"I'm gonna miss this 'will they, won't they' drama when I leave. You promise to update me?" Alice wasn't letting it go.

"You want me to text you every day to tell you that I'm single?" She smirked.

"No, I want you to text me *when* you start hooking up with Jake and give me all the dirty details."

Yeah, right. She's going to be waiting a long time for that message.

***

Saying goodbye to Alice was bittersweet. Although Lily was going to miss having her sister around, she was pleased to be getting her flat back. But before she could bask in the solitary hibernation she had planned, she needed to make it through the day.

Bluestone County's annual bake sale was afoot in the town hall. Lily had stupidly assumed she would just be able to pop in, buy some cake and disappear. Little did she know how misleading the name of the event actually was.

There were cake stands, drink stands, stalls and gaming booths, all of which spilled out from the town hall and into the cobbled streets. Teaming with locals, it was the busiest she'd ever seen the town since her arrival.

Everyone was there, including Sam and Jake, who'd found her within minutes. It was the first time she'd seen Jake since girls' night. Just as uncomfortable as her, they both relied on Sam to hold the conversation.

When Duke joined them, it started to feel more like a weird, messed-up double date. Lily participated in the games, but it was only the cake and drink getting her through the awkwardness. It was when Sam and Duke started to dance that Lily realised she needed to make a break for it.

Slipping into the crowd, she made her way back through the cake stands lining the street. Out of nowhere, she felt a hand clasp her arm from behind. Quickly spinning around, she saw Jake standing before her.

"They've blocked off that end of the road. Come on, I'll show you how to get out of here."

His hand dropped as he motioned for her to follow him. Feeling guilty she'd run away, she remained quiet as he guided her through the hordes. Soon, the crowds thinned, and the noisy chatter was a distant murmur.

Now that she could hear herself think, she broke her silence. "I'm sorry I didn't say goodbye. I just wasn't in the party mood."

"So, you weren't just avoiding me?"

Their pace started to slow as they neared the store.

Unsure of how honest to be, she felt herself pull at her fingers while contemplating how to answer.

"I was a little drunk the other night and said some things …"

"You wanted to know why I didn't kiss you." Jake came to a standstill.

Unprepared for his blunt answer, she found herself lost for words and unable to meet his eyes.

"If you still want to know why…" She looked up just long enough to see him shifting from side to side and staring down at his feet. "It's because I promised Sam that I wouldn't."

Finding the courage to lift her head again, she was now more curious than nervous. "You promised Sam you wouldn't kiss me?"

"Kind of, yeah. I promised I wouldn't hit on you."

"And why would you make that kind of promise?"

He attempted to hide his uneasiness with a short laugh. "Um, well, that's the thing. I'm pretty sure it has something to do with her not thinking I'm good enough for you."

It certainly didn't sound like the Sam she knew. She loved her brother more than anything. Any mention of him would be a chance to praise him. Maybe he was being polite. Maybe it was her who she thought wasn't good enough.

"Why would she think that?" Lily asked, their gaze still entwined.

Jake took longer to answer this time. As he rubbed the back of his neck, she could tell he was struggling to find the right words.

"It probably has something to do with my relationship history. Or lack of it." He paused. "See, I've never really had a long-term relationship before."

"Never? How long are we talking here?" She knew she was doing a bad job of concealing her shock.

"Um, maybe like a month or two."

"So, you've never been in love?"

His stare deepened as his expression became more serious. "Not yet."

Despite her attraction, red flags were flying all over the place. A thirty-five-year-old man who'd never been in love or had a relationship longer than two months, she was starting to see why Sam warned him off.

She couldn't look into his eyes any longer. It stirred

something inside of her that she wasn't ready to face. Starting to walk again, he slowly followed along beside her.

"So, you wanted to hit on me?" she joked, attempting to lighten the mood.

"And you wanted me to kiss you?" His tone turned more flirtatious.

"Um, that's not exactly how I remember it," Lily protested.

"Why don't you tell me how you remember it?" He poked.

"Hey, you were the one leaning into me, buddy!" she said as she let out a snicker.

"And what would you have done if I had kissed you?"

Twisting her neck, she caught a twinkle in his eye, complimenting his cheeky grin.

"I guess you'll never know."

As they approached the store, he tugged at her arm once again to stop her from going inside. This time when she spun around, she was met with Jake's heat-filled eyes.

Eyes that never left hers as his body moved closer and his head tilted down. "What if I want to know?"

Drowning in deep blue, it wasn't until she felt the warmth of his body pressed up against her that she realised she'd been pushed up against the window. His hands rested against the pane on either side of her head, crowding her and leaving her with nowhere to go, not that she wanted to leave. In fact, for once the voices in her head usually telling her to run were quiet. Instead, all she could think about was the smell of his musky cologne. Every breath she now took smelled of him.

Letting her lips part, as soon as his mouth touched hers, her heart thumped so hard it felt like it was pounding in her eardrums. What started as a gentle caress, quickly turned hungry as he pried her lips further apart to taste her. The more he explored, the more she panted and the hotter his touch became.

As his chest pressed harder into her, his hands moved:

one held her head in place while the other claimed her hip. Both drew her back to him every time she attempted to come up for air. No longer in control of anything, she surrendered to the weakening in her knees and let his strong hands hold her up while she let her fingers slide up the side of his shirt, circling every hard ripple she found.

But it wasn't enough; she wanted more. As she spiralled into a sensory overload, she knew she was already addicted. Addicted to the way he smelled, how he tasted, how he touched her, how he felt and even the sound of the guttural groans that she swallowed.

Just as things got blurry, a loud "ahem" broke them apart.

As Jake quickly removed himself from her lips and swung around, she immediately saw a disappointed-looking Sam and an embarrassed Duke over his shoulder. Even though they hadn't been friends for long, Lily recognised the look on Sam's face. She was mad. Really mad. All of a sudden, Lily's mind became a little less cloudy and the voice telling her to run was back.

So, after pulling down her top and catching her breath, she did what any sane person would do. She made up an excuse and got the hell out of there as fast as she could.

"Um … I need to get back to the store. Jessie's due a lunch break, and I promised I'd cover."

Purposely avoiding looking at Jake, she concentrated on Duke and Sam. Duke offered up a friendly smile while Sam continued to glare at her brother. Lily definitely needed to get out of there.

Taking the opportunity to run away unchallenged, she hastily scurried inside.

"Hi, Jessie," Lily could feel her voice shake.

"Hi, Ms. Lily," Jessie beamed back over at her as she continued cleaning the shelves.

"Please, Jessie, just call me Lily." She'd come to learn that the "Ms." was just a sign of respect, but it still made her feel like some sort of old spinster.

"I didn't know you and Jake were dating?"

Realising she must have witnessed the kiss, Lily mentally cursed. "Um, we're not. Officially. Um. It's complicated." What was she meant to say? Jessie was just a kid, barely eighteen; she had no idea just how complicated dating became after you hit thirty.

Jessie let out a gentle giggle. "Oh. Well, just a heads up. About a dozen people witnessed you guys kissing at the window. So, you might get a few more questions."

More mental swearing ensued. Of all the times to have a first kiss, broad daylight in the middle of town wasn't exactly ideal. The town rumour mill would be working overtime today.

After sending Jessie out to get some lunch, she slumped into the chair behind the counter. Jake, Sam and Duke were long gone, but she couldn't help but wonder what had transpired after she'd fled.

I should have stayed. I'm such a chicken.

Letting out a groan, she let her head fall into her arms resting on the counter. And that's when the flashbacks started. Why did the kiss have to be so good?

Why couldn't he be a terrible kisser and tried to bite me or swallow me whole or something?

She could still feel the graze of Jake's stubble against her cheeks. It was a good kiss. Too good. Nothing good ever came from a kiss like that.

The words "emotionally unavailable" and "womaniser" sprang to mind as she recalled their earlier conversation. What thirty-five-year-old man hadn't ever been in love? The wrong type of man, that's who. The type of man she always found herself attracting.

CHAPTER EIGHT

"Two weeks! Two weeks, Jake!" Sam shouted as she slammed the car door and stamped her feet against the gravel.

Jake started to miss the silent treatment he'd received in the car journey back to the ranch.

"You couldn't control yourself longer than two weeks?" She shouted after him as he circled round the car to face her.

He felt bad breaking his promise, but boy was it worth it. His heart was still pounding from the taste of Lily's lips and the touch of her silky skin. All he wanted to do was run back for more.

"Sam, how many times do I have to say I'm sorry."

"I don't know, Jake, especially now that I know your word doesn't mean shit."

He'd not seen her this angry since the time Brodie left a fence open, allowing one of their horses to escape.

"I like her, Sam. I like her a lot. I'm sorry I've upset you, but I'm not sorry I kissed her."

The flames behind Sam's eyes started to fizzle out as she gaged the seriousness of his tone.

Arms still crossed, she let out a huff. "You really like her?

Like more than a fling like her?"

"Yes, I do. I wouldn't have broken my promise if I didn't. I swear."

He didn't know what else he could say. He couldn't exactly promise her a happy ending, but he was well aware Lily wasn't the kind of girl you'd just have a meaningless fling with.

"If you hurt her …"

"I'm not planning to." Sensing it was now safe to come closer, he rubbed at Sam's arm to reassure her. "I wanna ask her out, on a proper date. Do I have your blessing?"

His sister was quiet for a moment. She took her time assessing him. Searching for what, he didn't know. He was telling the truth. Trying his hardest to be honest.

"Fine, but I mean it, Jake. If you hurt her, I'm gonna hurt you."

Sam stormed off into the house. He knew he needed to give her time to cool off, so he decided to make a start on his rounds.

On his walk to the stable to saddle up Rocky, Lily came to the forefront of Jake's mind again. Would she even agree to a date? Sure, she'd kissed him back, but she'd also run away again.

After mounting Rocky, he made his way down toward the creek. Thinking back to the kiss brought a smile to his face. It was one hell of a kiss. A kiss he could easily become addicted to. Maybe he already was. That would certainly explain the very real need to see her again suddenly overwhelming him.

***

It had only been a few hours since they'd kissed, but news of their tryst had already spread across the town. Just on his way over to the store, he'd been stopped three times by nosy neighbours wanting to know more.

His palms started to sweat as he made his way down the

crooked pavement. Why was he so nervous? He'd asked women out before, plenty in fact—why was Lily different?

Jake surveyed the store as he entered. She was nowhere to be seen.

"Looking for Lily?" Jessie squeaked.

"Hey, Jess, yeah, she about?"

"Upstairs. Go on up, I'm sure she won't mind."

After thanking Jessie, he took the stairs two at a time up to her apartment. One knock later and his heart started to race.

Lily glowed as she opened the door, a look of surprise encompassing her face.

"Can I come in?"

Waiting for her to decide, he observed her bite down on her lip, the obvious tell that she was nervous. Without saying a word, she nudged the door wider and gestured for him to enter.

"You want coffee or something?"

"Or something?" He smiled.

As he stood in the hall facing her, he had a sudden urge to kiss her for the second time. Her pouty lips parted as if she was thinking the same thing. Instincts now in control, he leaned into her and studied her reaction. The nearer he edged, the shallower her breaths became.

His finger softly tilted her chin up toward him, sending a waft of her spicy vanilla perfume straight to his lungs. Already drunk on her scent, he couldn't wait any longer to taste her again. His mouth covered hers and his tongue licked the seam of her lips until she opened for him.

Feeling her hands rest against his chest sent a rush of blood to his head. No longer able to think straight, he deepened their kiss and let his hands travel down to her waist. Gently guiding her up against the door, he drew her closer and suppressed a groan as she arched into him. The warmth of her skin enough to leave burn marks.

Letting his fingers slide under her vest, he heard her let out a soft moan. Hearing that sound did something to him.

Flipped an invisible switch. He didn't think he could want her any more, but he was wrong. His lust flared. He wanted all of her. But before his cravings could be satisfied, Lily pulled their lips apart. Her eyes still glossed over; she lightly pushed his chest back. She tried to catch her breath, still gazing deep into him.

"We can't," she declared through her gasps. "I can't."

His heart dropped. How had he managed to mess this up already?

"Why not?" He desperately searched her expression for answers. Hoping like hell she hadn't changed her mind about him.

"You've never had a relationship last longer than two months, Jake. I'd be a fool to just ignore that."

He cursed himself for letting that information slip, but he wasn't ready to give up just yet. After those kisses, there was no way she could deny what was there between them. She was just scared. He needed to try to reassure her. Edging closer, he caressed the side of her flushed cheek.

"You think I'm not serious about you, is that it? Cos you're wrong. I've never met anyone like you before, Lily. And I sure as hell have never felt like this." He felt more heat rush to her cheeks as he continued to stroke her.

"You think I've not heard that before, Jake? That's the oldest line in the book."

"It's not a line Lily. I mean it. I like you. A lot." His pulse started to race again as he looked deeper into her jade eyes. "Give me a chance to prove it. Go on a date with me?"

"Once we've crossed that line, it's gonna be hard to go back to being friends," she mumbled, now trying her hardest to avoid his gaze.

"I think it's safe to say we've already crossed that line." He tipped her chin back up toward him, forcing her to meet his eyes.

He softly brushed her lips with his once again, and in that moment he had his answer.

***

"I'm scared. I can't." Lily stood warily gripping Midnight's saddle.

A smile had been stuck on Jake's face ever since she'd agreed to go on a date with him, and it was still going strong. He liked everything about her. Even the fearful expression she was currently sporting while she studied Midnight.

Sam had let slip that Lily wanted to learn how to ride, so he thought teaching her would make the perfect first date. However, he hadn't taken into consideration how frightened she might be. He wanted her to have fun, not scare the daylights out of her.

"I'm sorry—I know you wanted to teach me, but I'm a little scared of being up there by myself." A look of guilt crossed her face.

"That's what you're scared of? What to do when you're up there?" he clarified.

"Yeah."

If that was the only reason, then it could easily be solved. He flashed Lily a wide smile as he began to remove Midnight's saddle. "Don't worry, if that's all it is, then we can work around it."

"What do you mean?" she asked cautiously.

"You can join me on Rocky." His head flicked over to his coffee-coloured companion. "It will give you a feel of what it's like, but I'll be in control. I'll make sure you're safe."

Lily started to fidget and pull at her elbow; he could tell she was still unsure.

"It's safe, I promise," he reassured her.

After helping her onto Rocky and unashamedly admiring the view, he positioned himself behind her. Being this close to her again brought back memories of their last kiss. It had been three whole days, but it was still all he could think about.

"Um, I'm starting to think you have an ulterior motive."

He let out a snigger. Her fear had certainly worked in his favour.

"Hey, I'm just passionate about teaching, darlin'."

A musical giggle vibrated into him. This was going to be fun. Tightening one hand around her waist, while he tugged Rocky's reign with the other, they began touring the ranch. Her muscles were still tense, so he started off slow.

"So, this how you teach all your guests how to ride?"

"Actually, Sam's the teacher. I'm just the tour guide."

"So, you don't make a habit of rubbing up against your guests under the pretence of a lesson?"

"Is that a hint of jealousy I detect?" His grin managed to stretch even wider.

"You wish."

He did. Pulling her further into his chest, he spoke softly into her ear, "Don't worry, darlin', you're the only woman I want to rub up against." Her breath instantly caught, and he couldn't help but feel smug at the effect he had on her.

Unable to see her face, he was relying on Lily's body language to do all the talking. So when he felt her slowly start to unstiffen, he couldn't be happier. But as she began to relax into him, her actions had the opposite effect on him. In fact, it sent his pulse racing. And just when he thought his heart couldn't pound any harder, he nestled his chin into her neck and inhaled her perfume.

Get your shit together, man. You're trying to prove to her that you're relationship material, remember? Not some horny perv who makes a habit of sniffing necks.

Snapping his head straight, he tried his hardest to focus. Turning his attention back to what lay in front of them, he guided them toward the creek. It was one of his favourite trails, so hearing Lily gasp at the beauty that surrounded them gave him a sense of satisfaction.

The longer they rode, the more relaxed she became. So much so, he passed her over the reins and whispered words of encouragement into her ear.

"I'm doing it! Oh my God, I'm doing it." Excitement

rang out in her voice as she slowly led them up a rise.

"Yes, you are, darlin'." Genuine pride bloomed in his chest. "Now, if you take us towards that tree over there"— he pointed ahead of them—"that's where we're gonna take a break."

Jake was first to hop off Rocky, offering out a hand to help Lily down and trying not to groan as she slid down his body. After tying up their ride, he led her a few yards farther into the foliage where he'd earlier set up a picnic for them.

"Did you make us food?" She turned then, a bright smile illuminating her features.

"Well, Ryan, our chef, may have helped."

As they made themselves comfortable, neither of them wasted any time tucking in. Ryan had outdone himself with this spread. Bottles of chilled root beer, pastries, cheeses, fruit and muffins all filled the basket in the middle of the blanket. He reminded himself to thank him later.

"So, is this the part of the date where you answer all my questions?" Lily flashed him a mischievous smile.

"Should I be scared?"

"That depends." He watched her slowly take another sip of her root beer, keeping his gaze.

"Yeah?"

"You remember what you said when you convinced me to come on this date … What were your words …?" Her eyes twinkled as she tangled her lower lip between her teeth. "Oh, yeah, I'll tell you anything you want to know."

What was it about this woman that made him lose his train of thought so quickly and apparently make all kinds of promises?

"And what is it you want to know, Lily?"

"Hmm, let's start with why you only date girls for two months."

Damn. She really wasn't going to let this go anytime soon.

"It's not like I planned it that way, darlin'. I've just never met someone I wanted to take it any further with."

It was the truth. She made it sound like he was some sort of player, stringing women along and then leaving them high and dry. But he wasn't. Maybe he was a little wild when he was younger, but the truth was he was sick of doing the casual thing. He hadn't been with anyone for almost two years. He did want a relationship, but he just hadn't found anyone he wanted one with. Not until he met her.

"So, you liked them enough to sleep with them but not enough to take them to a movie?"

Letting a snort slip out, he straightened himself up. "This really bothers you, doesn't it? Why, you think that's what I want from you? Just sex?"

"Isn't it?" she challenged; their eyes still locked on each other.

"No, Lily, it's not." He was at a loss; he didn't know how to convince her.

Breaking his stare, she moved her attention to the cluster of trees across from them. What he wouldn't give to know what thoughts were swirling around in that beautiful head of hers. It was obvious that his words hadn't reassured her.

"What are you thinking, Lily?"

Her eyes flicked briefly over at him before returning to the trees. "That I should be running for the hills."

"It bothers you that much?" A pit started to form in his stomach. Losing her now wasn't an option. He was only at the beginning of this, the beginning of understanding the feelings she was starting to stir up in him.

"Who gets to this age and hasn't been in love, Jake?" She met his gaze again. "I'd be an idiot to think that I'd be anything more than another notch on your bedpost."

Who even knew what love was? He didn't. But one thing was for sure, as much as he'd like to add her to his bedpost notches, he wanted her trust more. Which meant he had to convince her he was serious.

"Look, Lily." He moved the basket of food obstructing them and slid next to her. "We may have had very different relationship histories. You've been in love, I haven't. You've been in relationships, I haven't. But the fact remains that we're both still single in our thirties. Whatever it was we were doing, clearly wasn't working for either of us." A smile started to form in the corner of her mouth. "I may not be a relationship expert, but I'm pretty sure there isn't a guaranteed path that leads you to love. You just have to follow your heart and hope for the best."

"How can you follow your heart when you've never been in love?"

"Just cos I've never been *in* love, Lily, doesn't mean I don't know how to do it."

In that moment, all he wanted to do was kiss her. If he couldn't convince her of his intentions with his words, then he could show her. Show her that this was different, she was different.

He stroked a loose strand of her golden waves back behind her ear, then returned his fingers to her cheek, which was beginning to flush under him. His eyes narrowed on her tongue, which was slowly skimming her bottom lip, causing her pout to glisten. He couldn't resist her any longer.

Catching her lips with his, he gently brushed them apart and delved deeper. Strawberries and root beer lingered on her tongue, the sweet taste only intensifying his cravings. His fingers travelled back into her silky hair, allowing him to pull her into his hold.

Sparks flew off them as she used her hand to slowly torture him, letting it slide up and down his chest while he struggled to breathe. Trying to keep control, or that was at least what he told himself, he clasped hold of her waist and tugged her closer.

Holy shit. I am so fucked.

CHAPTER NINE

Lily stared down at the phone again; Jake's name was still flashing. It must have been the tenth call she'd ignored since their date two days ago. It wasn't that it was a bad date, quite the opposite. But something wasn't right; she just didn't trust it, didn't trust herself.

Jake had heartbreaker written all over him, and if their kisses were anything to go by, it wouldn't take long for her to fall hard for him. She just needed some time to let her feelings for him fizzle out.

Leaving her phone on the sofa, she slid back down onto the floor and continued to fish through the last of Matt's boxes. She pulled out more pictures—her eyes lingered on one of him fishing. Was he fishing at the ranch? A few photos later, her suspicions were confirmed as she came to a photo of him with Jake. She wondered why Jake hadn't mentioned that before.

Letting out a sigh, she rolled her head back. Maybe Jake knew more about the kind of man her dad was than he was letting on? *Stop thinking about him.* Pushing her thoughts of Jake aside again and ignoring the goosebumps starting to prickle on her skin, she carried on rummaging in the box.

"What the hell?" she muttered to herself as she reached

for a large stack of letters.

Her heart stopped as she realised they were all addressed to her. Why were they here, and why hadn't he sent them?

She picked up the first letter and immediately noticed *return to sender* scribbled across it. More and more questions trickled out like syrup. Did her mum know about the letters? Was she the one to refuse them? Why didn't he try and send them again?

Her hands started to shake as she unsealed the envelope.

Dearest Lily,

I hope you received the doll I sent you. They said it was the most popular one at the toyshop. If you like it, I will buy you more and bring them over when I next visit.

What? What on earth was he talking about? Adrenaline pumped through her veins as confusion struck. But before she could read any more, a bang on her apartment door made her jump.

Forcing herself up, she went to see who it was. As she swung the door open, she was met with the sight of an angry-looking Jake.

Shit.

"What's wrong?" His fury quickly moulded into concern. "You look like you've seen a ghost?"

She had, sort of. Feeling numb, she stepped aside to let him through. Avoiding Jake didn't seem to matter anymore, not when she had a whole load of other emotions to deal with.

"My dad ..." She could feel her voice tremble. "I found some letters." She gestured toward the box on the living room floor. "He wrote to me."

Jake looked back and forth between her and the stack of papers on the carpet. After a gentle stroke of her arm, he made his way over to the pile and picked up the letter she'd been reading.

She followed him over, and when her knees started to buckle, she slumped into the squeaky leather sofa. Moments later, Jake bounced down next to her.

"I don't understand. Does this mean he didn't run?" His baffled expression matched the feelings churning inside of her.

"Maybe, I don't know. I need to read them all. Try and figure it out."

She recognised the look on his face. Sympathy with a side of pity mixed up with adorable concern.

"Have you eaten?"

"What?"

"You heard me, darlin'. Have you eaten today, or did you forget again?"

I forgot to eat a couple of times and now he thinks I can't take care of myself! But he's right, isn't he? You haven't eaten, have you?

As if he'd read her mind, he said, "You read. I'll make us some food." After gathering the rest of the letters, he placed them next to her and walked over to the kitchen.

Taking a deep breath, she mustered the courage to pick the piece of paper back up. She attempted to quieten her thoughts; her questions would just have to wait. She needed to read everything before coming to any kind of conclusion.

Every word she read left behind an ache. Even the mundane descriptions of her father's week twisted her insides. But it was the mentions of visiting her that caused her eyes to swell. Everything seemed to suggest that he hadn't abandoned her. Questions began to bubble again.

"Okay, time for a break." Jake removed the paper from her grasp and gently slid his hand into hers. "I've whipped up pancakes and there's a fresh pot of coffee with your name on it."

He lightly tugged her to her feet and led her over to the breakfast bar in the kitchen. The sweet waft caused her stomach to groan; she was suddenly aware of how empty it was.

She took a seat while Jake finished pouring them coffee and pushed the plate in her direction.

"Thank you. You didn't have to do this."

There was that smile again, the one that made her knees

weak and her stomach flutter.

"So, you learn any more from the letters?" He leaned over the counter and took a sip of his drink.

"Um, just more questions, I guess. I just don't understand why I didn't get any of them. I think I need to talk to my mum. Surely she wouldn't have sent them back without showing me?"

Jake's face wasn't exactly giving her confidence that was the case. And he didn't even know her mother. Who was she kidding? Of course she could have. But why?

Shaking her head, she sought comfort from her sugary pancakes.

"I've been trying to call you. For a few days now."

Fuck.

A lump started to form in her throat. She felt unprepared; she thought that she would have a bit longer to think up a good excuse.

"Um, yeah, I'm sorry." Nothing useful sprang to mind, only the truth. She let herself go quiet to see if a simple apology was enough.

"So? Do I get to know why?" Apparently it wasn't.

Damn, she would have to tell him. Taking another bite of her pancakes for luck, she fidgeted on the stool before meeting his gaze.

"I, um, I ..." A sigh slipped out while she tried to organise her words. "I don't know if us seeing each other is such a good idea."

She looked for signs of shock or disappointment, but his face remained the same.

"Because you're scared." That was a statement, not a question. Pulling up a stool, his eyes remained on her. "I'm not gonna hurt you, Lily. How can I show you that?"

It was true; she was scared. Scared that even now, staring into his eyes, he had the ability to rip out whatever was left of her heart. And it was already in pretty bad shape.

"No offence, but I've dated guys like you before. You know, charming, attractive, say all the right things ... and then, a few months down the line, when they've got what they wanted, that's when the pain begins. And every time it happens, I lose a piece of myself. I just don't think I'm strong enough to go through it again."

Sloping off the stool, she made her way back to the sofa, her honest admission surprising even herself. No more lies, no more excuses, she'd had enough of that to last a lifetime.

Jake's hand caught her before she reached the living room. Spinning her around, his wild eyes were burning into her.

"I'm not one of those guys, Lily. I promise you that." She let him jerk her further into him, his hand slipping to her waist. "I'll prove it to you."

"Oh yeah? And how exactly are you going to do that?"

He dipped his head until their faces were just inches apart. "I'm not gonna have sex with you." His deep voice rumbled.

"What?" She stifled a giggle.

His smirk tipped to one side. "No sex," he repeated. "We date, get to know each other and take sex completely out of the equation."

"And that will accomplish …?"

"It will give you the chance to realise that I'm not the guy you think I am."

The warmth of his now shallow breath curled her lips. "What about kissing?"

"I think you know the answer to that."

Accepting his touch and his challenge, she met his mouth halfway and surrendered to his embrace. Her mind became misty as her senses were now overpowered by the taste of him on her tongue.

***

It had been days since she found her father's letters, and she still hadn't worked up the courage to call her mum. One more night wasn't going to make a difference, she told

93

herself again as Jake clasped her hand and led her inside the French bistro. Feeling the familiar tingles shoot down her spine as their fingers laced together, it was clear she had other things to worry about right now.

Jake's conditions had certainly intrigued her. She liked the idea of waiting; it would allow her time to get to know him better while offering her some emotional protection.

As they settled into their surroundings and placed their orders, she could feel his penetrating stare before she even looked up.

"You look beautiful tonight, Lily."

She loved the sexy way her name rolled off his tongue.

Offering him up a smile, she scanned the crisp white shirt that stretched across his broad chest. He wasn't going to make this easy on her. It was almost as if he knew exactly how much she wanted him. And with that knowledge, he knew what to do, say and even what to wear to torture her.

"Thanks. You're looking pretty good tonight too."

His smile widened as the waiter poured their wine. Why did he make her so nervous? They'd already kissed, yet there were times she felt like a timid teenager trying to talk to her crush.

She lunged for her glass as soon as the waiter had left, needing some relief.

"I want to know everything about you."

Almost choking on her wine, she let out a cough. "Um. Everything?" She gulped. "Could you be a little more specific?"

"What's London like? You grow up there?"

Realising he was being serious, she had no idea where to start. Her life wasn't that interesting, in fact, it was so uninteresting that the most exciting thing she'd done was leave it all behind.

Sure, tell him that, that doesn't make you sound like a loser at all.

"There isn't much to tell. London's great and everything, but when you grow up there, I don't know, it's just different. People get all excited about the city, but after thirty-two years of living there, I was just kind of sick of it. Everything that I used to love about it slowly turned into things I hated about it."

"Like what?"

"The crowds, the built-up streets, the people." She stopped to think about her morning commute and being barged out of the way by grown men. "Everyone is in such a rush, y'know?"

"So, you came here for a slower pace of life?"

"Honestly. I don't know why I came here." She took another sip of her drink. "I just wasn't happy there."

"Well, there's definitely no crowds in Bluestone ... or built-up streets."

"And the people?" She raised an eyebrow.

"From what I hear, they're charming, attractive and say all the right things." His eyes twinkled as his smile turned cheekier.

He was smooth. Too smooth. Those sparks flying off him were going to set her alight and burn her to the ground.

The flirtatious comments kept coming, and by the time the food arrived all she could think about was when he was going to kiss her again. She needed to distract herself. It was time to turn the tables and learn a bit more about him.

"Tell me something about you that no one else knows." She took delight in watching him squirm.

She let him mull while she dug into her boeuf bourguignon. Eventually, he cleared his throat and set down his cutlery, a wide-eyed grin pasted across his face.

"Okay. When I was twelve, I stole the keys to my dad's truck and drove two towns over. I was gone for like six hours."

"And no one noticed? Not even Sam?"

"Nope, not even Sam. Even to this day she doesn't know." His grin faltered as he paused for a moment. "I went looking for my mom. It was just after she moved away."

A pang of guilt hit her. She hadn't heard the full story from Sam, but she'd noticed the pain strain her voice

95

whenever she mentioned her mother.

"Did you find her?" she asked cautiously.

"No."

Happy he'd opened up a little, she pushed for more. "So that's when she took off, when you were twelve?"

He nodded. "Sam didn't tell you?"

"No, I think it's still too painful for her to talk about."

Then why are you pushing him to?

She watched him take a big gulp of his drink and waited until he was ready to continue. "She moved to Bluestone from the city. Got married, had kids, but evidently it wasn't enough for her. She hated being a rancher's wife and fled back to the city when I was twelve."

"After she moved away, did you see her again?"

Jesus, Lily, give him a break.

"A few times, not often. My dad had full custody." He started to fidget. "Do you mind if we change the subject?"

Maybe she shouldn't have pushed him, but curiosity got the best of her. She quickly blabbered on about the store until he started to relax again.

When she'd finished her meal and laid down her cutlery, her gaze flicked back up to find his stare roaming over every inch of her. A glint in his eyes that insinuated he knew exactly what she was thinking.

"What?" she asked.

"I know there's something you wanna ask me but you're too afraid. Go ahead. Ask it."

What the fuck? First off, how did he know? Second off, cocky much?

"Hmm." She took another swig of her wine, ignoring the scorch marks his gaze was leaving on her skin, pondering whether she really wanted to know the answer.

"Time's up. Go on, ask it." His confidence niggled her. Enough for her to come to a decision.

"Okay, Romeo. You said to me the other day that this"—she motioned between the two of them—"this was different. Different from your one-month, two-month flings. Why are you so sure of that? You barely know me. For all you know I could be an axe murderer on the run from the law. How can you possibly know that I'm someone you'd want something more with?"

He didn't attempt to hide his amusement. "You really did date some assholes back in England, huh?"

Why was that funny? "Your point?"

"You have no idea, do you?" He shook his head. "You wanna know why this is different, why I'm so sure? You're special, Lily. And I'm not just talking about your looks. Yes, you're stunning, but you're also funny and smart and you don't take any shit. You're the kind of woman wars are fought over."

Fuck me, that's a good answer.

As she stared into deep blue, she felt her heart start to race. Okay, now she needed to kiss him. If she could get away with dragging him across the table, she would do just that. How the hell was she supposed to get through the rest of dinner now? Or more dates for that matter?

ISOBEL REED

CHAPTER TEN

Jake winced as his phone bellowed out again. It wasn't a dream like he'd initially thought, and whoever was ringing him was clearly not giving up. Craning his neck, he glared over at his clock; it was just gone midnight.

Who the hell is calling so late?

Eyes still filled with sleep, he opened them just enough to answer.

"What?" he groaned into the speaker.

"Jake? Hi, it's Teddy," a sheepish voice replied. "Um, I'm sorry to ring you so late, but I didn't know who else to call."

Suddenly alert, Jake's heart started to thump against his ribs as his thoughts spiralled. Teddy would only be calling so late if it were bad news. Immediately thinking the worst, his sister and Lily were at the forefront of his concerns. The idea of anything happening to them made him feel nauseous.

After he'd managed to sit up and clear the sleep from his throat, he didn't waste any time finding out.

"What is it, Teddy? What happened?" Impatience clearly creeping into his tone.

"Um. It's Lily." The line went quiet as Jake's palms

started to sweat. "She's a little … um how do I say it … She's a little worse for wear."

"She's drunk?"

"Yeah. Wasted. And I thought maybe you ought to come on down."

Thank God.

Even though he was relieved it wasn't something more serious, he was struggling to wrap his head around why Lily would be drunk at Mickey's on a Wednesday night. Especially when she hadn't mentioned any plans to go out earlier when he spoke with her, nor had his sister.

After hanging up, he jumped out of bed, pulled on his jeans and continued to ponder. Lily didn't seem like much of a drinker. In fact, if anything, she was a bit of a lightweight. The one time he'd seen her tipsy was at his sister's girls' night on two or maybe three small glasses of wine.

Maybe that's it … She had a couple of drinks and accidentally got hammered?

Once he'd parked outside, he noticed Lily straight away as he slung open the doors. And as soon as he caught sight of her draped over the bar, clinging to a half-empty bottle of whiskey, he knew he was wrong. This wasn't "three glasses of wine" drunk; this was "does she need her stomach pumped" drunk.

Meeting Teddy's gaze and giving him a nod, Jake blew out a long breath as he approached her.

"Hey there, darlin'." He gently caressed the side of her exposed arm that lay on the bar.

She jolted up and twisted, a blurry-eyed look of anguish across her face. "Jake? Of course. Of course you called Jake." She momentarily glared over at Teddy before swinging back around to him. "Go home, Jake. I don't … I don't need saving," she stuttered.

She was wasted all right. And angry as hell. What had happened? He would kick the ass of anyone who had the nerve to upset her. All of a sudden, he felt the urge to fix it, fix her. If she let him, he'd do anything to see that beautiful smile back on her face. But first he needed to get her out of here.

"How about I take you home, sweetheart?" He reached for the bottle she was clutching, but she quickly pulled it into her.

"No. This is mine!" She cradled it into a hug. "Get your own!"

He tried and failed to suppress a chuckle.

Cute and angry.

"Okay, darlin', how about we take the bottle with us, huh?" He arched over and placed his hand on her back to see if he could encourage her to move.

But she pushed him away again. "No, Jake." Her voice was louder this time. "I told you, I don't need saving." He watched on as her hands started to flap, so much so he was worried she might accidentally throw herself from the stool. "I'm a … I'm a grown-arse woman, not some fucking … d-damsel in distress!"

Now he really was worried. What had happened since he last saw her yesterday and kissed those sweet lips goodbye?

Teddy eyed him from across the bar. It was late and the last of the barflies were long gone. Despite finding the obvious humour in the situation, Jake knew Teddy was more than ready to go home and get some sleep. Jake needed to hurry this removal up. He knew what he had to do; she just wasn't going to like it.

"Okay, darlin', let's get you home."

With one fell swoop, he picked Lily off the chair and swung her over his shoulder into a fireman's lift. The bottle she clung to was now being struck across his backside as she shouted and wriggled for him to put her down.

"Thanks, Teddy. Night, Teddy." He nodded as he made his way to the door, ignoring her cries.

"You put me down, Jake McAllister! I swear to God, if you don't put me down—"

"Yeah, yeah," he cut her off. "There'll be hell to pay."

By the time they reached the store, not only was his ass hurting from the bottle beating, but his eardrums weren't doing great after listening to Lily's very loud protests. Using her helpful positioning over him, he managed to retrieve her keys after rifling through her jean pockets. Which unsurprisingly earned him more bashes from the whiskey bottle.

Pacing up the stairs, it wasn't until they were safely in her apartment that he let her down. Which turned out to be a mistake. As soon as he did, he was met with several pushes to the chest.

"I don't need saving." She continued to slur, before tripping over her foot and dropping to the floor.

"Jesus, Lily." He quickly dived to pick her up, lifting her to her feet. "You drink the whole damn bar?" This time he was only met with a groan.

She was going to have a sore head tomorrow, that was for sure. Resigned to the fact that he wasn't going to get a whole lot of sense out of her tonight, he decided to try and put her to bed so she could sleep it off. In the interest of safety to avoid any further falls, he picked her up again, but this time he held her tightly against his chest. As he carried her to her bedroom, she mumbled something about doormats.

"Let's get you to bed, sweetheart," he whispered soothingly in her ear in an attempt to calm her.

After carefully placing her on the bed, he slipped off her shoes and took a seat on the edge next to her. Looking a little less like she might punch him, he risked a touch of her soft skin and trailed his fingers down the side of her cheek. Smoothing her hair out of her face, he revealed that irresistible pout again.

"I want my whiskey … You're supposed to drink it until the pain goes away." Just the thought of her being in any type of pain ripped through him. As he continued to caress her, he noticed her eyes begin to mist. "It's not gone away," she whimpered, and soon a tear dampened his finger.

"Shh, it's okay, sweetheart. Whatever happened, we will fix it together. It's gonna be okay; I promise."

Why didn't she call me?

He'd do anything to take her pain away, anything. Maybe tomorrow she would tell him how.

"It's time to get some sleep, darlin'."

He rose slightly to pull the sheet over her, then went back to stroking her until her eyes fluttered closed. Once he was satisfied she wouldn't leap up and run for the whiskey bottle, he stood, but before he could even take a step, her hand reached out and dragged him back toward her.

"Stay. Please," Lily whispered.

He could feel himself smile. There was nowhere else he would rather be.

After toeing off his boots, he crawled under the covers next to her. To which she responded by turning away from him and shuffling backward until she came to rest in his lap so he could spoon her. He let out a short but quiet laugh as she made herself comfortable. He could get used to this.

***

Lily had been on his mind all day. It had been so hard leaving her this morning. She looked so peaceful in her sleep, and even though he wanted to drown her in kisses first thing, it was more important that she get some rest. So he slipped out.

He'd spent all morning checking his phone hoping to hear from her, but nothing. Sick of waiting, as soon as he was done with his chores, he made his way down to the store.

It was closed when he arrived. He wondered if it had been closed all day. She'd drained half the bar last night, so chances were high that she'd slept through opening.

As he approached the door, a smile crept over him at the sound of music blaring. She was dancing it out. A warm feeling settled in his stomach. Goddamn, she was cute as hell.

After banging on the door, he waited patiently for a peek of that pretty, flushed face.

"Jake. Hi. Um … come in." As predicted, her cheeks were pink. Looking a little wary, Lily stepped aside to let him in. "Listen … about last night …"

"I'm surprised you remember." His eyebrow raised.

He took a moment to drink in the image of her. Her wild hair was tied up into a messy bun, and to his delight, she wore yoga pants and a clingy grey T-shirt that highlighted all of her curves. It was official. He was smitten.

Letting out a nervous laugh, she rubbed behind her neck. "Yeah, I'm not gonna lie, it's a little bit blurry. I'm sorry if—"

He cut her off and suggested they head upstairs. It was doubtful he was going to get any answers while they stood in the middle of the shop floor. After a quick nod, he followed her upstairs.

Once they were inside, he encouraged her to sit down while he made them some coffee.

When he returned, she'd made herself comfortable and was sitting cross-legged on the squeaky leather couch. Passing her over a mug, he took a big sip of his drink before launching into questions.

"So, you gonna tell me what happened yesterday?"

She started to fidget and looked down into her cup. "Um … yeah. I'm really sorry that you had to come and get me. I'm so embarrassed."

Feeling the need to reassure her, he instinctively reached over and tipped her chin up and stared into her solemn eyes. "Hey. No need to be embarrassed, darlin'. Wanna tell me what happened?"

"I had a big fight with my mum, and I guess I decided to drown my sorrows."

"In whiskey apparently."

Her head tilted again as she looked back at her drink. "Oh God, I'm mortified. I don't even know how much I had to drink; everything's still so blurry. Do I want to know what I did?" She met his gaze again, rosy pink splotches staining her cheeks.

He felt bad for grinning, but he couldn't help it as he thought back to her hugging the whiskey bottle. "Well, let's just say, the next time I carry you out of a bar, I'll make sure you don't have a bottle to beat me with in your hands."

"Oh no. I didn't?"

"You wanna see the bruises on my butt?" He chuckled.

Her free hand went to her face. "Oh my God. I'm so sorry. I'm never drinking again."

Unable to resist the urge to comfort her, he placed both their mugs on the coffee table and pulled her into his arms until her head lay against his chest. He lazily stroked his fingers up and down her back while she snuggled into him.

"I'm sorry, Jake. The last thing you need after a long day's work is to come rescue my drunken arse."

"But it's such a nice ass, darlin'."

"Ha. Ha. Seriously, though, I'm sorry—it won't happen again."

Dipping his chin, he rested it on top of her head and breathed in the irresistible scent of her coconut shampoo.

"What happened with your mom?"

"I asked her about the letters. It turns out she's spent the past thirty-two years lying to me." Lily's voice began to shake. "She's the one who sent the letters back."

Jake's heart sank. That's why she was in so much pain last night. The thought punched him in the gut. He wished he could take all the pain and sadness away from her. Instead, he tightened his grip on her and continued to let his fingers trace her spine.

She was quiet for a minute before declaring, "I feel like an idiot."

"What? Why?"

"Cos, I blindly went along with everything she told me. Not questioning whether it was true or not. Who the hell knows what else she lied about? And, really, I'm an adult.

An adult who could have come out here sooner and asked the questions I needed to ask. Find out for myself why he really left. Now … now it's too late."

He felt his shirt dampen as she released her tears.

"Hey." He moved his hand so he could thumb away her tears. "Don't do that. Don't punish yourself like that. You had no reason to doubt what your mom told you. Shoulda, woulda, couldas don't mean shit."

"But now he's gone. And I'll never know him or hug him or have a relationship with him." More tears dripped, each one sending a pang to his chest.

"It's okay, Lily. I've got you. It's okay." He went back to caressing her, trying his hardest to soothe her as she cried into him.

It was almost too much to bear, seeing her so upset and not being able to do anything about it.

They remained quiet for a while, so quiet he heard the exact moment Lily's breathing started to sync with his own. He had no idea how long they stayed like that. Tangled. Minutes or hours. It didn't matter though, and he didn't care. She could lay in his arms forever for all he cared, anything to make her feel better. Besides, who didn't want to cling on to perfection? Getting high on coconut waves and feeling heat bloom in his chest as she snuggled deeper into his hold.

When she finally drew back, he instantly missed her. "I'm sorry, Jake. I didn't mean to just fall apart like that." She was back to avoiding his gaze. Which gave him the perfect excuse to touch her again.

His hand gravitated toward her face and gently angled it back up to him, feeling his heart skip a beat when he got a look at the sadness still clouding her eyes. "I want to help. What can I do?"

After a defeated shrug, she covered his hand. "Thank you, but it's okay. I don't need saving, Jake."

***

I don't need saving, Jake. What the hell did that mean anyway? She'd thrown those words at him drunk and now sober, yet he still had no idea what she was talking about. He wasn't trying to save her, he just wanted to help. Why wouldn't she let him?

Pulling up to the ranch, he let out another sigh. He hadn't wanted to leave, but Lily had insisted she needed some time alone. He just hoped she was going to call her sister and not spend the night by herself, crying. Just the thought of her crying without him there to comfort her did something funny to him.

Slipping out of the truck, he made his way into the house. All the lights were on and a delicious smell was drifting in from the kitchen. Was Sam cooking? Following the smell, he regretted not announcing himself as soon as he saw Sam and Duke making out against the counter. Thankfully, they quickly jumped apart at the sight of him.

"Brodie said you were over at Lily's tonight. Everything okay?" Sam enquired as she readjusted herself and pretended to check on the food.

"Um, yeah, I went to check on her. She's umm … she wants to be alone tonight. Don't worry, though, I'm just gonna grab something to eat and I'll leave you guys to it."

He made his way over to the fridge. A simple sandwich would do him.

"What did you do, Jake? Did you upset her? I swear to—" Sam waved her spatula at him accusingly.

"I didn't do anything," he snapped, disappointed at the lack of faith she had in him. "She had a fight with her mom, okay? Wow. Nice to know what you really think?"

"Oh, don't sulk, Jake. You haven't exactly got the best reputation with women. You can't blame me."

How do you know? It's not like you've ever met anyone I've been with since high school.

He was getting sick of these sweeping accusations and insults. Trying to let it go, he chose to ignore her. Reaching for the bread, he went to work on making his food so he could get out of there as quickly as possible.

Duke patted him on the back. "Go easy on him, Sam. We can all see he's crazy about Lily."

Apparently the conversation wasn't over. Although he appreciated Duke's defence, he was still pissed off with his sister, who should give him more credit. How could Sam possibly think he would hurt Lily? Sure, he wasn't exactly an expert in relationships, but he hadn't intentionally hurt anyone. In fact, he had gone out of his way to make sure any woman he'd been with knew he only wanted something casual. But Lily was different. Lily was the first woman he'd met where he wanted something more. Something real.

"Yeah, I know." Sam exhaled as she nestled into Duke's chest. "I'm sorry, Jake. I just want you to be happy. Lily too."

An apology? Now that, he wasn't expecting. He didn't know how Duke had done it, but he'd never seen his sister so mellow and happy before. She definitely didn't usually make a habit of apologising either. Whatever he was doing, Jake just hoped he kept doing it.

Shooting a smile over at the lovebirds, he decided it was time to leave them to it. "Thanks, sis. Enjoy your dinner."

Avoiding bearing witness to another make-out session, he grabbed his sandwich and went back out the way he came. Taking big bites as he went, he made his way to his favourite spot down by the creek and took a seat overlooking the water.

Lily was the only person he'd ever brought out here. The view made him think back to their dance and the light in her eyes as she spun into him. The memory made him smile so wide that he felt his cheeks stretch.

Pulling out his phone, he had the urge to speak to her. They hadn't arranged their third date yet, it hadn't felt right to ask her while she was upset, but now he was regretting not asking. Trying to respect her space, he decided to message her instead of calling.

Jake: Jessie covering the store on Saturday?

He stared into the phone until he saw the three dots appear.

Lily: Yep, why?

Jake: We're having a party for the guests at the ranch, will you be my date?

He felt like he was back at school as he waited for her reply. It was their third date and they'd already kissed plenty, so why did he still feel like this? Why did she have such a strong effect on him?

Lily: Sure :) what time?

Perfect. All he had to do now was plan a party.

CHAPTER ELEVEN

Lily paced up and down the shop floor. Moving around helped. It kept her from calling her mother and screaming at her again. She couldn't shake the anger. When she'd first spoken to her mum, she was upset more than anything, but the more she thought about it, the angrier she became.

She'd spent the past few days reflecting on her childhood. She was always the sensible one, the dependable one, and it had dawned on her that she'd spent her whole life catering to her mother's wants and needs instead of her own.

"Well, no more," she reminded herself as she settled back behind the counter.

She was still feeling restless, but she was more determined than ever to make the store successful. The opening sale had been great, and she'd had a steady stream of customers since, but she still wasn't making a profit.

Convinced she needed to expand her customer base, she'd decided to set up an online store. She'd managed to find a website builder that was simple enough for her to understand, but it was taking a lot more time than she'd thought to make a half-decent-looking site.

Delving back into her laptop, she had just finished

adding her first product when her phone vibrated across the counter. Peering down, she saw Alice's picture flash up.

"If you're gonna tell me to ring Mum, I'm gonna hang up."

"Lily, come on. She's beside herself." Lily groaned into the phone but kept her mouth shut, "She's called me crying five times already today. You need to speak to her."

"No fucking way, Ali. She can cry her crocodile tears all she likes. She's a manipulative cow." Her heart started to race just thinking about her. The last thing Lily needed right now was to talk to her mother.

Alice let out a sigh. "I know she fucked up. *She* knows she fucked up. But you guys can't go on like this forever. What are you gonna do? Not talk to her for the rest of your life?"

"I'm too angry to talk to her right now, Ali. I just can't." Her eyes started to swell again. "I need time."

"Not even to hear her out?"

"There's no excuse." Lily puffed. "Dad wanting to move to another country doesn't give her the right to stop him from contacting me. And then lying to me about it all these years. What would you do, Ali … if it were your dad?"

The line went quiet. She knew exactly what Alice would do if the roles were reversed. She'd hit the roof. After a minute she heard her exhale again.

"I get it, Lily. You have every right to be mad. Just promise me you will speak to her when you cool off?"

What exactly was the forgiveness period for lies and betrayal? Speaking to her mother again in the imminent future was definitely out of the question, but she felt bad leaving Alice to pick up the pieces.

"I'm sorry, Ali. I can't promise I'm gonna cool down anytime soon. Y'know, being out here, being away from her … I don't know how to describe it, but I feel more like myself. For the first time ever, I feel like I'm finding out who I am." She paused, trying to find the right words. "Mum likes to try and control us, she always has. And when she didn't have much luck with you, I was the one who bore the brunt of it. I'm not that person out here. I'm not just some doormat."

"You're not a doormat," Alice chimed. "No one ever thought you were a doormat."

"Come on, Ali, of course I was. Good ol' Lily will do it. All the stupid fucking errands I did for that woman, I was like her personal secretary—not her child. No wonder she didn't want me to leave."

"She loves you, Lily. I do too. So does Dad. I know she's not perfect. I mean, she drives me up the fucking wall too, but she loves you so much and she really is upset. She's scared she's going to lose you forever."

As angry as Lily was, the thought of her mother upset still stung.

"I can't speak to her right now, but can you tell her I will? Eventually. Tell her I need time. Please?"

Alice reluctantly agreed before hanging up. It was the best Lily could offer.

***

Why was she so nervous? Why did Jake still make her knees weak after two dates, several kisses and even a drunken rescue?

She looked down at her dress again as she waited outside the door. Alice had been appalled that she only had one dress and had left her this one. Lily suddenly felt self-conscious. It was a simple strappy sundress, but she realised Jake had only seen her in a dress once. Would he think she was overdressed?

Before she could tie herself up in knots any further, the front door swung open and Jake's wide smile was all over her.

"Damn, Lily." His gaze crawled up and down her outfit. "You look hot."

The heat in his eyes caused her stomach to flutter.

Instead of inviting her inside, he took a step forward, entering her space. Butterflies soon turned into somersaults as he inched even closer, gently moving his hand up her neck and into her hair. Within seconds his lips covered hers and pried her mouth apart.

Surrendering to the sweet relief of finally having her thoughts silenced, she allowed herself to get lost in his touch. Deepening their kiss, Jake's free hand clasped her hip and dragged her toward him. As she pressed her hands into the wall of muscle that made up his chest, the no-sex agreement flashed through her mind. Whose stupid idea was that?

The more her fingers explored, the hotter she became. Tracing each muscle made her long to discover what lay beneath the stretched plaid. But before she could travel underneath, he slowly pulled away. Still close enough to feel the warmth of his breath, he rested his forehead against hers and stared into her.

"I've missed the taste of your lips." His smooth, husky voice sent goosebumps all over her.

Needing another fix, she brushed her lips back over his, allowing her tongue to savour one last taste before gently tearing herself away.

"I've missed you too," she whispered, swallowing her urge to go back for more.

"I could kiss you all day if you let me, darlin'."

"I don't know if that's such a good idea." She laughed as she imagined just how long she would last before ripping his clothes off.

He stroked the side of her face again and then allowed his hand to move down her body, skimming her curves under the sundress. "You're probably right. I'm not sure I'd be able to trust myself."

She watched as his lips curved into a smirk, the fire in his eyes still visible. Then his hand reached for hers. "Come on, the party has started."

Leading her around the house and into their famous

barbecue spot, Lily saw a dozen tables piled with food and drinks. Music was blasting from large speakers atop a makeshift stage and some of the guests were already dancing.

"So, what's the party for?"

"Um … it's just something we do for guests every now and then." He tugged on her arm and led her to where the guests were dancing. "Can I have this dance?"

Seizing the opportunity to get close to him again, she happily agreed.

It took a total of two songs for all her insecurities to resurface. She'd been so wrapped up in family drama all week that she'd forgotten the effect Jake had on her. And how hard she was falling.

"You've got that serious look on your face again, darlin'. What's going on in that pretty little head of yours?" he whispered into her ear, making her shiver.

Nuzzling her chin into the curve of his shoulder, she kept her gaze in front of her. "So, this is our third date, right?"

"Yeah?"

"How many dates do you think it will take for me to know?"

She felt herself smile as his chuckle vibrated against her chest. "Are you asking what I think you're asking?"

"That depends … what do you think I'm asking?"

He pulled his body away to see her face but made sure he still kept a firm grip on her waist.

"I think you're asking when we can end our agreement."

Back were those blue flames.

Trying to hide her sudden shyness, she let out a giggle and broke his stare. But within seconds, in a classic Jake move, his fingers lightly pushed her face back toward his. His grin widened as he waited for his answer, but no words were coming out of Lily any time soon.

"How many dates do you think it will take for you to trust me?" he asked, his expression becoming more serious.

"I … I don't know yet," she mumbled as she turned her face away again.

Drawing her back into him, he continued to sway them. It was a good minute before he spoke again.

"I'm not going anywhere, Lily. I'm a patient man."

Closing what little distance there was between them, Lily rested her head against his shoulder. Every part of her longed to trust him, but his past still niggled her. She wasn't naïve enough to believe she was special or different from all the other women he'd been with. Who's to say they weren't just like her and trusted too easily only to have their heart broken?

Whistles forced her head back up. Sam. Of course. Drawing back, Lily exchanged a smirk with Jake before they untangled themselves.

Moments later, they were sat at one of the picnic tables with Sam and Duke. Lily was quick to refuse the wine Sam was offering. She opted for a soft drink instead and expertly ignored the knowing grin Jake flashed her.

It was kind of sweet to watch Sam and Duke together; they were clearly still in the honeymoon phase if the wandering hands were anything to go by. Lily itched to know more. After a few looks and a rather big hint, Sam and Lily excused themselves to go inside to use the bathroom.

Back in the house, Lily jumped straight into the questions.

"So, tell me everything. Are you guys official?"

Sam beamed over at Lily as she sank into the sofa. "Yeah. He asked me to be exclusive and we … you know?"

Lily let out an excited shriek. "Oh my God, you guys are so fricking adorable! So … was it good? Is he as good in the bedroom as he is in the barn?" She wiggled her eyebrows.

They both burst into laughter as Sam's cheeks pinkened. "Lily!" she protested before burying her head in a throw pillow. "I'm not gonna answer that!"

"Okay, okay. No talking then, just one nod for yes and two for no?"

Sam slowly lifted her head from the pillow and nodded once before giggling again.

"Enough about me and Duke, what about you and Jake? You guys can't seem to take your eyes off each other."

As much as she wanted to confide in Sam about all her insecurities, Jake was her brother and it didn't feel right.

"I like him—we're taking it slow."

"Slow as in ... you're making him wait?" Nothing got past Sam.

Lily could feel herself blush. "I feel weird talking about this with you. He is your brother, Sam."

Giving her a friendly nudge, Sam was having none of it. "Don't be ridiculous, you're my friend. I want you to be able to talk to me about anything. Just pretend he's a random guy and I don't know him, not that I want to hear about any kinky sex stuff. Keep that to yourself."

More giggles ensued. "Okay. But, honestly, there isn't much to say. We really are taking it slow and getting to know each other."

"Okay, but you like him, right?"

"Yeah. I do. I really do."

"I sense a but?"

Lily took a moment to decide what to and what not to say. "Well, you know about my relationship history, right? I'm not exactly good at all this stuff. In fact, it's safe to say that I'm fucking awful at it. So going slow seems sensible."

Sam went quiet. When she started talking again, she looked unsure of herself. "Is it cos of his relationship history too?"

Lily nodded.

Of course it is! I'm scared shitless that he just sees me as a challenge and once he's got what he wants from me he will ghost me.

Not able to voice all the neurotic thoughts vying for attention, Lily remained quiet.

"Look"—Sam placed her hand over hers—"when I found out he liked you, I warned him off." Ignoring Lily's eye roll, she continued. "But then you guys kissed, and after that … there was no way he was gonna listen to me. But, honestly, I've never seen him like this before, Lily. He likes you a lot."

"Did you warn him off because of his past?"

"Of course I did, Lily. You think I'd let him hurt you? He may have only done casual in the past, but he promised me *this* was different. And you know what, after seeing the two of you together, I believe him."

Sam's words made Lily feel a little better. Sam was his sister after all. If she thinks whatever it was between them was different, then Lily had no reason to doubt her.

Once they had wrapped up their gossip session and Lily had learnt a rather interesting fact about today's party, they made their way back outside and joined Jake and Duke. Both men were now standing and chatting with the other ranch hand, Brodie.

As soon as she was back beside Jake, he took no time wrapping his arm around her waist. In an almost possessive way. It was a simple, subtle move that had her grinning like a Cheshire cat. Even the dull ache she'd felt in her heart all week was starting to subside.

Just as the sun was beginning to set, Jake stole her away from the others and led her back toward the creek.

"So, you put this all together in a day?" She smirked as she slid closer to him on the bench.

"Sam told you?" He let out a soft laugh and bounced his leg a few times.

Holy shit, is Cocky Jake nervous?

It was probably the most vulnerable she'd seen him, which made her feel slightly guilty for enjoying it so much. "You know, party or no party, I would've come over if you'd asked me to."

Jake stared off into the distance. "I wanted you to feel comfortable, especially after the week you've had—I thought maybe a group setting might help you to feel more at ease."

Is this guy for real?

"That's probably the sweetest thing anyone's ever done for me." She turned to face him.

His eyes flicked back to hers. "I'd throw a party every day for you if it put a smile on your face."

She didn't know whether it was the words he spoke, or the smouldering look he gave her, but like a moth to a flame, she immediately sought his soft lips. Pulling him close, as her tongue started to explore, she let the world around them slip away.

***

The next day, Lily was attempting to finish uploading the products to her new website when her mind went back to Jake. She had an idea, one which would hopefully allow her to get to know him better as well as her dad.

Picking up her phone, she dialled his number, but it went straight to voicemail. Figuring he was probably on a trail or doing chores, she left him a message.

Hey, Jake, it's Lily. So, I had an idea, and I need your help. You know how I was saying that I wanted to get to know what kind of guy my dad was ... Well, I know that you guys were friends and I get that he wasn't much of a talker... but I was thinking maybe we could do some of the activities you did when you used to hang out with him— maybe doing the things he liked to do will help me understand him a bit better? Anyway, call me back when you get a chance.

Letting out a sigh, she sunk back into her chair and pulled the laptop back onto her knees. She didn't know why finding out what kind of person Matthew was meant so much to her, but it was all she could think about since she read his letters. Was she like him? Jake hadn't shed much light on their friendship, but they were clearly close enough that he entrusted him with keys to the store.

Diving back into her work, it wasn't long until she was distracted again. This time she was back to thinking about Jake. They'd spent most of last night glued to each other's lips, making her feel like a horny teenager. Not only were his kisses painfully addictive, but they made her realise just how deep her feelings were becoming. There was only one person who she could confide in.

"Ali, I need your advice."

"Well hello to you too!" Alice snickered down the other end of the line.

"Ali, please, I need your help. I've been trying to do this bloody website all afternoon, but I'm too distracted. I need to talk some stuff out."

"Okay, okay, is it Mum?"

"No, it's Jake."

Alice squeaked down the phone. "Ooo, Yummy Jake. So, let me guess, you guys are getting it on and you're freaking out?"

"Not exactly. We've been on three dates, and I like him but ... we have this kind of no-sex agreement."

"What the fuck? Why?"

Lily went on to explain Jake's reputation and the fact that he'd never been in love. At least Alice recognised that they were red flags too.

"Okay, you're dating, no sex, so what's the problem?"

Lily pushed the laptop back onto the table and crossed her legs on the sofa. "The problem is ... I like him, a lot. Too much. I think even with the no-sex pact, he has potential to really hurt me, and I'm scared."

"Oh, Lilypad," Alice tutted before pausing. "Look, I understand, I do ... but you can't let the fear of getting hurt stop you from living your life. Yes, by the sounds of it, Jake doesn't have the best track record, but the fact that he's told you about it and is going out of his way to make you believe what you have is different—it says a lot."

"So, you're saying I should just go with it and forget about his past?"

"What I'm saying is ... you can't change the past, so why let it ruin the present? You like this guy, Lily, and he likes you. Forget all the other bullshit and listen to your gut. You wanna shag him—shag him."

They both fell into giggles, talking about it was helping. Alice was pretty wise for a younger sister.

"Okay, okay. I'm not gonna just shag him after three dates, though, Ali. I need to get to know him better. I'm not going to let my hormones make all my decisions ... not yet anyway."

After divulging every detail of the past few dates and reliving her embarrassingly drunken encounter, Lily was finally feeling better.

And her mood only improved further when she hung up and saw that she had a message from Jake.

Jake: Sorry I missed your call. I was clearing out the stables. Sounds like a plan. I'll pick you up for fishing tomorrow—be ready by 4:30 a.m.

What kind of maniac went fishing at four in the morning?

CHAPTER TWELVE

The dusty orange sky lit up the ripples as the light breeze ruffled the leaves in the tree hanging over where they rested. Jake glanced over at Lily again as they sat along the bank holding their fishing rods.

Going by her grumpy greeting this morning, he'd already established that she wasn't a morning person, yet she still managed to take his breath away before the sun had even risen.

"Am I allowed to talk?" she whispered, her mouth turning up at the sides.

"Of course. So how do you like fishing? Relaxing, right?"

He'd never taken a girl fishing before, another first for him. More often than not he was alone, not that he minded, but there was something to be said for having company, especially if that company was Lily.

"Actually, yeah, there's something about it, something therapeutic almost. Don't get me wrong, this is still a ridiculous time to be awake, but I get why you like it."

He could easily get used to seeing that smile every morning, whether there was fishing involved or not.

"Does that mean you'll come fishing with me again?"

Her smile widened and lit up her eyes. "I think you could

twist my arm."

If he'd learnt anything from their last date, it was that he needed to resist the urge to kiss her as often as he liked. Kissing her only left him thinking about one thing, and as much as he cursed himself for coming up with their agreement, he was a man of his word.

"So, how often did you and Matthew fish?"

"Maybe once or twice a month. He knew it was something that I used to do with my dad, after my dad passed away... Matt asked if he could join me now and again."

Lily looked off into the distance. "What did you guys talk about?"

Jake tried to think. The truth was that Matt was a man of few words and most of their conversations revolved around what they were doing in that moment. He couldn't help but feel like he was letting Lily down by not being able to tell her anything useful.

"Nothing deep, I'm afraid. Just boring stuff, like how the store was doing, how the ranch was doing, stuff like that." He watched the hope across her face fade and felt his heart ache for her. "He'd never been very talkative ... but you could tell his heart was in the right place."

This time her smile didn't reach her eyes. After tucking her golden waves behind her ear, she stared into him again. "So, what other stuff did you guys used to do?"

The thought of Lily mucking in with the chores was enough to make him chuckle. "Um ... he used to help out around the ranch now and again, said a hard day's work cleared his head."

"You're messing with me?"

Holding his hands up, he continued to laugh. "I swear! But y'know if you're not up for it, darlin'..."

Unable to wipe the smirk off his face, he keenly studied Lily as she arose and placed her rod on the ground. A gust of vanilla made his mouth water as she sauntered over to him and positioned her legs on either side of his. Feeling his pulse start to race, he bit down on his lip as she carefully took a seat on his lap.

"Oh, I'm up for it."

So much for resisting her. Before he had a chance to think, his hands were on her back and drawing her closer to him.

Dipping her head, she caught his bottom lip and gently ran her tongue across it. Shivers immediately ran down his spine, unleashing something feral from within.

Letting out a low growl, he couldn't wait any longer to claim her lips and pry her apart. Which was exactly what he did next. Savouring every sensation her taste on his tongue unleashed, his grip tightened around her as fire filled his veins.

Needing to touch her, he found himself reaching under the hem of her vest, but before he could explore her silky soft skin, the chair buckled. With an almighty thud, they were pulled to the ground and the flimsy chair frame protruded into his back.

Luckily, his tight grip had shielded Lily from any harm, but he did a quick scan of her to double-check. When he finally met her gaze, he relaxed, and within seconds they'd erupted into laughter.

***

Jake returned Rocky to the stable and began grooming him. Once the dirt in his hair was loosened, he brushed it away. The repetitive strokes had always helped to quieten his mind, but today he was finding it harder than ever to stop it racing.

After his early morning fishing trip with Lily, his mom, Laurie had invaded his thoughts. It had been almost a decade since he'd ended their bi-annual visits, but he was starting to wonder if he'd made a mistake.

Rocky nuzzled his nose in Jake's neck. "What do you think, bud? You think I should call Laurie?" Giving him a tender pat, he continued brushing.

Life was short. Matt's death had taught him that. The man was fit and healthy one day and dead from a heart attack the next.

Ever since Jake had found out about the letters, he hadn't been able to stop thinking about his mom. And why she left. Lily's relationship with Matt hit too close to home. But unlike Lily, he had a chance to make things right. Or at least hear his mother out.

After saying goodbye to Rocky, the grumble in Jake's stomach led him straight toward the on-site restaurant, where he hoped the last of the guests had dispersed after the lunch rush. Ryan was taking his break on one of the whitewashed wooden tables when he arrived, sipping on his afternoon espresso.

"Smells damn good in here, man. Anything left?"

Peering up from his newspaper, Ryan looked pleased with the compliment. "Sure, there's plenty in the back. Help yourself."

Making a beeline for the kitchen, Jake took no time filling a plate with biscuits, roast beef, beans and potatoes. Just the hearty smell caused him to salivate.

Ryan offered up a seat as Jake re-entered the dining area. Happily joining him, he took off his hat and wasted no time tucking into his food, satisfying the rumbles in his stomach.

"I saw you and Lily getting close at the party—are you guys a thing?"

Taken aback by the sudden questioning, Jake finished chewing before answering. "Um yeah, I guess we are. Why?"

"No reason, man, I was just thinking of asking her out myself, but it looks like you beat me to it ..." Ryan trailed off with a nonchalant shrug.

Jake wasn't expecting that. Although he shouldn't be all that shocked. Why wouldn't Ryan be interested in Lily? Lily was beautiful and Ryan was single, a similar age, and from what he'd seen, popular with the ladies. He swallowed down the jealousy that had already started to make his muscles tense and made an extra effort to censor his expression as he met Ryan's gaze.

"I didn't know she was your type, man. Don't you normally go for brunettes?"

Ryan let out a snort. "As opposed to you—who goes for everyone?"

Seriously? Why does everyone seem to have an opinion on my love life all of a sudden?

Not only was that not true, but that was exactly the kind of talk that would send Lily running. And the last thing he wanted was to lose her.

"Come on, man, that's not funny. I like this girl, a lot."

Ryan took in his expression and the lack of humour on his boss's face and decided to change tack. "I was just kidding around, man. I'm happy for you. She seems like a nice girl."

Jake nodded once, hopefully conveying that this conversation was over. It worked. Ryan was up and out of his chair a minute later, but not before imparting more words of wisdom.

"Just don't fuck it up, yeah?"

Jake just sighed. He didn't need a reminder. That was exactly what he was trying not to do.

***

Chores were definitely more fun with Lily by his side. It had been almost a week since they'd seen each other, and he'd been surprised by how much he'd missed her. Busy with the store and her new website meant they had to wait until the weekend to see each other because that was the only time that Jessie could cover.

Despite her long week at work, she was true to her word and arrived at five in the morning to start a full day's work with him at the ranch. Her determination to understand more about what kind of person Matt was, was impressive.

They started the day by cleaning out the stalls, checking the water tanks and feeding the horses. It was now time to groom them before taking them out for some exercise.

Jake's eyes kept wandering back to Lily; she was a natural with the horses. Letting them nudge and lean into her, she seemed at peace while she stroked Midnight.

"She likes you."

Lily beamed back at him. "I like her too. She's so affectionate."

"Not with everyone she's not. She trusts you."

Lily caressed her again and whispered into her ear.

"So, you gonna ride her today … or join me on Rocky?"

"Umm … I think I need a few more lessons before I go at it alone." Looking unsure of herself, she broke eye contact and turned her attention back to the horse.

He shouldn't be so pleased that she wasn't up for riding alone, but the thought of holding her tight in his arms again set his pulse racing.

Once they'd walked all the horses, he got his wish. After saddling up Rocky, he helped Lily up and eagerly slipped into a position behind her. Coconut, vanilla and sugar overwhelmed his senses as he pressed further against her. He could get drunk on her scent.

Taking the reins, he made sure she was safe in his arms before they began their ride.

"So, where are we going?" He could hear the excitement in her voice as they started to gallop.

"We need to check the fence lines. I hope you're comfortable because it's gonna be a long ride."

Riding with her this time felt different. The first time they'd ridden Rocky together, she'd been so nervous, even to lean into him. But today, she was relaxed and comfortable enough with him to let him hold her tight.

He let her take the reins as they patrolled the fence lines and tried to keep his focus on the task in hand as his fingers slipped under her top and rested against her creamy skin. Just touching her sent him into a sensory overload. He'd never wanted someone so much in his life.

"Are you trying to distract me?" She snuck a look at him over her shoulder, a mischievous grin lighting up her features.

"What?" He pretended to act shocked. "I'm just making sure you don't fall off, darlin'."

"Oh, really? So, your hands underneath my top are for safety reasons only?" She giggled.

"That's right, sweetheart." He continued to caress the silky skin under her vest and dipped his head to pepper kisses along the curve of her neck. "Just keeping you safe."

Taking great pleasure in the way Lily's body reacted to his touch, he let himself indulge a little longer before finally dragging his lips away from her. It was too easy to get carried away. She triggered a primal instinct in him no one else had ever unearthed. All he wanted to do was make her his, so he could protect her and keep her safe.

For the rest of their ride, he did his utmost to distract himself from the texture and taste of her skin. He chose safe conversation topics like the website and their new guests.

By the time they'd finished checking the fences, it was lunchtime. Once they settled Rocky back into the barn, he took her hand and escorted her back into the main house. He may not be a gourmet chef like Ryan, but he could rustle them up some sandwiches.

Once they'd brought their food outside and settled into the patio chairs, Jake took the opportunity to tell her about his mom.

"There's something I wanted to talk to you about."

Lily's green eyes widened as she brushed crumbs from her mouth. "Yeah?"

"My mom, Laurie … I've been thinking about her a lot lately." He stole a glance at Lily, immediately recognising the sympathy across her face. "It's been a while since I've seen her, and I was thinking of changing that … and making a trip up to the city."

The air went quiet as Jake tried to squash the emotion

that had taken over his voice.

"How long has it been … since you've seen her?" Lily edged closer and rested her hand on his knee.

"We used to see her a few times a year when we were kids. Dad used to take us up there. But the older we got, the less frequent the visits. The last time I saw her was about nine, ten years ago."

Lily's jaw opened and closed a few times before any words came out. "Wow. Um, I take it you guys don't talk on the phone or anything?"

Go on, tell her. Tell her that you ignore all your mom's calls and messages and watch her run for the hills.

There wasn't an easy answer, and he wasn't sure she would understand the truth, so he opted for a condensed version of it. "She's tried to get in touch with us a few times, but the older Sam and I got the more we realised what she'd done. Does that make sense?" He covered the hand Lily had placed on his thigh and laced his fingers through hers. "It got to a point where I just didn't want to see her anymore."

"You were angry. I get it."

Of course she did. If anyone was going to understand it was her.

"I just stopped taking her calls." He met her eyes once again. "I don't know if it's got something to do with you and Matt, or if I'm just missing my dad, but she's been on my mind. If I were to go to Billings next weekend—to go see her—would you come with me?"

Unable to hide her shock, she squeezed his leg. "Yes. Yes, of course I will. But what about Sam?"

"I already spoke to Sam, she uh … she doesn't want any part of it."

Lily stared at him a little longer and then leaned into him, quickly wrapping her arms around his waist. Unprepared for her embrace, he was stiff in his seat, but that didn't stop her, in fact, she hugged him tighter. Even though he wasn't used to this kind of affection, he had no complaints. As his body melted into hers, he enveloped her and couldn't imagine ever wanting to let go.

ISOBEL REED

CHAPTER THIRTEEN

Lily finished packing her overnight bag and took a seat on her bed. It had been a week since she'd agreed to go to Billings with Jake, and this morning they were going to make the journey there. She wasn't a fool; she knew spending a night away with him was playing with fire. It already took all of her willpower not to strip off and throw herself at him every time they kissed. So she had no idea how on earth she was going to survive a night in a hotel with him.

She bit her fingernail again, a habit she thought she'd quit long ago that had recently resurfaced with a vengeance. The truth was, she'd already fallen for him. Her heart was already compromised. Sex or no sex, she knew he was already in a position to break her.

A knock on the door forced her out of her head. Jake was here—there was no turning back now.

Looking as handsome as ever, he'd paired his stretched blue jeans with a tight, fitted white T-shirt. Her eyes quickly darted to his perfectly sculpted chest, which was practically begging to be touched. She found herself shaking her head in an attempt to shake off her dirty thoughts.

"You okay?" Jake asked, clearly concerned by her odd choice of greeting.

"Yeah, sorry. I was just thinking about Jessie. I hope she'll be okay alone this weekend."

Liar!

What was she supposed to say? *Actually, just the sight of you is making me want to say hell with the agreement, drag you to my bedroom and then chain you to my bed.*

"All covered. Sam is going to check in today and tomorrow. No need to worry." There was that smouldering smile again. *Not helping.* "Come on, let's go."

Thankfully, she managed to get some sort of control over her hormones on the drive over. And the drive itself went quicker than she thought. Even with their now nightly phone calls, they managed to talk their way through the three-hour journey.

In that time, she'd learned all about his horrifyingly bad taste in music, his twinkie addiction and exactly why he was kicked off the football team in high school. In turn, she'd shared some of her own stories and the many occasions she and Alice managed to get themselves in trouble while they were growing up. And maybe a few times when they were old enough to know better.

Jake was meeting Laurie for lunch, so the plan was to check into the hotel before he went to meet her. Although he'd asked her to join them, she thought it was best he handle their first meeting on his own. He was planning on seeing her again tomorrow before the drive back, so if all went well, Lily could meet his mum then.

It still touched her that he wanted her there. She liked this side of him, and she had a hunch that he didn't let many people see it.

The hotel was even nicer than the pictures. There was something so grand about American hotels. The rooms seemed so much bigger and more elaborate than she was used to. Jake had booked them adjoining rooms, to ensure she didn't feel pressured. She appreciated the sentiment, but the idea of spending the whole night cuddled up with Jake was becoming more appealing by the second.

After leaving her bag on her bed for the night, she took advantage of the connected rooms and paid Jake a visit.

"This place is amazing, Jake. Have you seen all the toiletries? Would you judge me if I brought them all back with me?" She grinned as she bounced down next to him on the bed.

He let out a deep laugh, and with one arm, he pulled her into him. "I'll do you one better, I'll let you take mine home too."

Moving her hair out of her face, his laugh came to a stop, but his smile remained in place. "Lily"—his eyes fixed on hers—"I want you to be mine."

The word "what" slipped out while she tried to gather her thoughts.

"I want to make this official. I guess thirty-five-year-olds don't have girlfriends, but that's essentially what I want you to be. My woman ... exclusively." She was still trying to decide whether it was a statement or a question when he continued. "I might have called you that a few times this week, and I realised that I forgot to actually ask you if that was okay."

Her heart and her head finally agreed on something. As much as it still scared the shit out of her, there was no denying she wanted him. "Yes, I want that. Does that mean you're mine?"

"Damn fucking straight, darlin'," was all he said before taking her lips. His kiss was slow and soft, making her body tingle and her heart skip. But before they lost control, Lily pulled back. It was time for him to meet Laurie.

***

Lily spent her time alone multitasking. In between checking her phone and her laptop, she was also managing to successfully freak the fuck out.

Even though they had technically been dating for a month, was that enough time to be able to trust him? She spent the next few hours overanalysing every single detail of their relationship so far but remained confused. Two months was his longest relationship, and they were still a good four weeks from breaking that record. Would she be a fool to sleep with him this weekend?

Her head was still spinning when Jake returned. She searched his expression for a clue as to how it went, but she struggled to read it.

"So ... how did it go?" She patted the bed next to her, gesturing for him to sit.

He let out a sigh as he plonked onto the super soft mattress. "It actually went okay. I said everything that I wanted to say to her and ... she listened."

"And?"

"And, for the first time she explained stuff from her point of view. It wasn't exactly what I wanted to hear, and I'm still not sure I exactly understand it, but ... I don't know, I feel like it helped to hear it."

A wave of relief flooded over her. "I'm so pleased, Jake. Do you feel better? Indifferent?"

His grin shot to the corners of his eyes. "I feel good. I'm glad I came."

There were so many more details that she needed to drag out of him. With that in mind, she suggested room service for dinner so they could stay and talk in the room and eat in his bed.

Once she'd heard a little more, Lily seemed to finally grasp why Laurie had left. After ending things with Jake's dad, she wanted to move back home. But neither of them liked the idea of uprooting their children, so it had been agreed that Sam and Jake would stay with their father, and she would visit on weekends.

Obviously, regular weekend visits turned out to be not so regular. And her reason for that being that she worked weekends was pretty lame in Lily's opinion, but it was what it was. Sadly, that distance Laurie had put between her and her kids resulted in not only a strained relationship but one that was much harder to salvage now that they were older.

Although it was probably hard to hear, Lily was happy Jake had finally got some answers. The truth wasn't always pretty, but maybe now that he knew, he could move on. Maybe even begin a new kind of relationship with his mother, on his own terms.

As the hours passed, their empty plates were discarded, and she'd found herself snuggled into Jake's chest. But being this close, listening to his heart thumping in her ear, she started to crave him. It had been too long since they last kissed. And she wanted to change that. Lifting her head from his shirt, she licked her lower lip, hoping he'd take the hint.

In less than a second his mouth was on hers, his tongue sweeping into her mouth, making the hair on her arms stand to attention. But it wasn't just his mouth making it hard to think, his big hand was running down her side, his thumb lightly grazing her breast as his fingers explored the curve of her waist.

She surrendered to the fuzziness, a feminine whimper escaping her lips as she let her own hands travel across his heaving chest and drag down his hard torso.

Just as she was getting ready to lose herself in him, he slowly pulled back, and she found herself gasping for air. "We have to stop," he stated, his gravelly, masculine tone making her want to do anything but.

"Why?" she whispered, already painfully aware of the answer to come.

"Because I can't control myself when you kiss me like that, darlin'." The bright blue flecks in his eyes glowed in the orange light.

She swallowed down the lump in her throat. She knew he was right. "Nor can I ... when you kiss me like that." She caught another glimpse of the heat in his eyes. "You're right. I'm not ready yet. But do you think ..." She stopped, unsure that it was such a good idea.

"What?"

"Do you think we could sleep in the same bed tonight?" The idea of being in the room next to him and not in his bed felt wrong.

"Of course, as long as you promise to keep your hands to yourself, sweetheart." One wink and a playful smirk later and she was back in his arms.

Pleased she hadn't packed her unicorn pyjamas; she used her room to get changed into her cream satin shorts and vest. Once she'd brushed her teeth and wiped away what was left of her makeup, she found Jake already half naked in his bed.

Holy shit he looked good. Even her daydreams hadn't done his abs justice. He looked like some sort of underwear model. This was going to be way harder than she thought.

Before she slipped under the covers, she noticed his eyes all over her. The satin nightwear was definitely the right choice. Although after seeing what lay beneath his clothes, she couldn't help but wonder if she matched up to the usual women he went for. Surely this drool-worthy beast of a man could have anyone he wanted, why was he settling for a boring plain Jane like her?

He let out a low whistle as she covered herself under the sheet. "Jesus, Lily, you look so fucking good."

How did he do that? With one look, he could turn her to mush and make her feel like the sexiest woman in the world. Pushing her insecurities to the back of her mind, she let herself smile and bask in the way he made her feel.

"So, fair warning. Obviously, there are some things as a man I can't control." There was that mischievous smile again.

Giving him a playful push, she let out a chuckle. "All right, cowboy, I don't need a birds and the bees talk, it's time to sleep."

***

Lunch with Laurie wasn't as awkward as Lily had

thought it would be. Laurie reminded Lily so much of Sam it was scary. The hardest part of the weekend turned out to be spending the whole night in bed with Jake and fighting off every urge that coursed through her.

The journey back went even quicker than the drive there. They talked mostly about Laurie and Lily's impression of her, and eventually Jake opened up a bit more about his childhood. In particular, what had gone through his mind when he'd stolen his dad's truck and gone out looking for his mum. Just the thought of a sad and confused twelve-year-old Jake made her heart squeeze. But now that she understood him better, she felt closer to him.

Sam played on her mind the entire ride home. Would Sam ever consider having a relationship with her mum? One thing Lily was all too aware of was that no family was perfect, but you do your best with what you have. She pondered talking to Sam about it, but the last thing Lily wanted to do was get in the middle of more family drama. Especially as she was still in the midst of her own.

By the time they got back to Lily's apartment, the sun was starting to set. While she should be getting straight back to work and letting Jake have an early night, she had other plans.

After a long, knee-melting kiss goodbye, Jake turned to leave. But before he even took a step toward the stairs, Lily reached for his arm and pulled him back.

"Wait, don't go. I want you to stay ... the night."

"You mean?" His puzzled expression quickly turned curious.

"Yeah." She bit down on her lip a little too hard, suddenly feeling nervous.

Jake edged closer and tilted his head to the side. "But back at the hotel, you said you weren't ready?"

Feeling herself gulp, she tried to steady her voice. "I wasn't then ... but ... I am now." She made herself hold his gaze. Blue flames flared in his eyes.

It was silly, but by spending the night curled up together,

not having sex, she realised that she was ready to have it. She'd been an idiot to think that she would somehow be protecting herself by not sleeping with him. Not after this weekend. It was crystal clear that she was already gone for this man. And she was done torturing herself.

Without saying another word, his head dipped and within seconds he was prying her lips open. A potent mix of musky cologne and his own masculine scent hit the back of her throat, stimulating her senses and blurring her vision.

With one fell swoop, he lifted her off the ground as if she weighed nothing and angled her legs to wrap around his waist. His tongue continued to sweep inside her as he booted the door shut and carried her into the bedroom.

It was only after he placed her down and toed off his boots that their mouths broke apart. And she missed his taste instantly. Feeling her breath become shallower by the second, he leaned until his forehead was pressed against hers. It was then that he traced a finger down the side of her face, his lips following the line down the nape of her neck where he kissed, sucked and nibbled until every nerve in her body felt like it was on fire.

With her brain suddenly hazy, she felt his hands drop. They brushed down her, exploring every dip until they reached the hem of her top. Slipping it up slowly, even her overheated skin felt hotter as his fingers slid over her. Lifting her arms long enough for him to cast the top aside, a moan left her lips as his mouth roamed further down her body.

"You're so damn sexy, Lily." His words vibrated against her skin.

Needing to touch him, she ignored the sound of her heart pounding in her ears and reached for his shirt. He helped her tug at the buttons, matching her urgency, until material was finally ripped from him and she was left with the sight of hard ripples. But she didn't get a chance to touch them, because he was pulling her back into him, his lips finding hers again. Skin on skin pulsating against each other as his tongue delved deeper.

She couldn't even tell if she was still breathing as more garments were tugged and pulled until they, too, hit the floor. The feel of his hard flesh against her softness stoked a fire in her belly. One so fierce she was beginning to suspect they were close to burning the whole damn place down.

With her senses fully overwhelmed, Lily's only coherent thoughts were that no one had ever touched her like this. Or made her heart race so fast that she thought it might explode. And just when she thought he couldn't possibly kill off any more brain cells, he lightly ran his hand along her thigh. Circling across her skin, slowly moving inward. Just as she let out a gasp, he broke away from her lips to whisper into her ear.

"Let me make you feel good, Lily."

CHAPTER FOURTEEN

Lily spent the next day in a daze. Every now and again a memory of the night before popped into her head, causing her cheeks to flush and her fingers itch to call Jake. How was the man single? There was nothing he wasn't good at … and that body, just thinking about it made her swoon.

"Shit."

Abruptly closing her laptop, she realised she was running late. At least her website was now live. Now all she had to do was let Rob work his marketing magic. After fumbling to put today's takings in the safe, she quickly locked the back office and grabbed her keys.

Sam was already at the diner when she arrived. Once she'd given her a big hug, she slid into the red leather seat opposite her. It had been almost two weeks since they'd caught up at the party and in between work, Jake and Duke, they hadn't had a chance to see each other since.

"So, Jake tells me you guys are official now," Sam excitedly beamed as she slurped on her shake.

Lily had no idea why hearing that made her so happy, but she did her best to hide it. "Yep, he asked me over the weekend."

"I have to admit, I was a little dubious at first, but, damn

... I think this is the happiest I've ever seen him."

"Yeah?" Lily couldn't wipe the smile off her face even if she tried.

"Yeah! We can all see he's crazy about you. You know he was whistling all morning? Whistling, Lily!" Sam let out a chuckle.

"I'm pretty crazy about him too." Saying it out loud was scarier than she thought it would be, but it was too late, there was no turning back now. "Anyway, enough about me—I want to hear everything about you and Duke."

A milkshake, fries and some ice cream later, Lily was up to date on Sam and Duke's relationship and even managed to squeeze out all of the dirty details that led to a permanent smile being plastered across Sam's face. Were all cowboys so talented, she pondered?

"So, did Jake tell you about Laurie?" Lily braced herself for the worst, she knew it wasn't her business, but it felt like the elephant in the room.

"I already know what you're going to say, Lily. No, I don't want to see her."

"Trust me, I get it. Matthew left me too, remember? It's too late for me to get to know my dad, but it's not too late for you to get to know your mum."

"It's not that simple." Sam's eyes grew misty. "She didn't want us, Lily. She left us without a mom when we needed one the most. Who does that?"

Lily reached out and placed her hand over Sam's, giving her a gentle squeeze. "I'm not saying it's not a shitty thing to do, it is. But this isn't about her, it's about you. I think you should hear her out. If you still feel the same way after, then that's okay; at least you'll know that you tried. And maybe you'll even get some closure."

Sam pulled her hand away. "What about your mom? You gonna hear her out?"

Lily deserved that. Sam was right. Who was Lily to tell Sam to talk to her mother when she had spent the past few weeks going out of her way to avoid speaking to her own?

"I'll tell you what, if you call your mum… I'll call mine?"

Sam scoffed, a single eyebrow lifting. "Fine. I'll think about it. Can we drop it now?"

Thinking about it was way more than Lily expected; she'd totally take that.

***

Determined to make the flat feel more like home, Lily was taking advantage of Jessie being able to cover the store mid-week. She was spending the day cleaning, decluttering and unpacking some of the new homewares she'd purchased online.

After working up a sweat moving her bed from one side of the room to the other, she dropped onto the mattress to catch her breath.

"Another bloody box?" she grumpily mumbled to herself as her eyes caught the sight of a brown box where her bed used to be.

Dragging herself off the cotton sheets, she went over to pick it up and hauled it back onto the bed with her. The box was a lot smaller than the others she'd found. Once she'd peeled back the tape, she peered into it in disbelief.

"What the actual fuck?"

She studied photo after photo, her heartbeat growing wilder. How could her dad possibly have these? These were pictures of her. He must have had one of her at every age up until she was eighteen. How was this even possible? Letting the photographs slip through her fingers, her gaze went to an envelope, the only other item in the box.

Flicking it over, she immediately saw her name on the front. Ripping it open, her hands began to tremble. She pulled out a single sheet of paper with messy writing scrawled across both sides.

Dear Lily,

If you're reading this then it means I never did get a chance or the courage to say what I need to say to your face.

She tried to steady her breathing and forced herself to continue.

I know it may not mean much now, but I want you to know that I'm sorry. Sorry for not being there for you or being the father you needed or deserved.

When I came to Bluestone, I hadn't planned on staying, but I did. I could go on about how I fell in love with the place and the people, but I'm not sure that's what you want to hear. The truth was I never felt like myself in London. I'm not like your mother. I hated the city, the crowds, the chaos. When I came here, for the first time in my life, I felt like I was home. Maybe it was the connection I felt to my birth parents, or maybe it was because I could finally hear myself think. Either way, I couldn't bring myself to leave.

Bile trickled up her throat. She felt like she was going to vomit, cry and pass out all at once. So that was it? He didn't like city life, so he upped and left his wife and kid? Was he being fucking serious? She felt her blood start to boil. Her mum was right. Biting back her anger, she made herself read the rest.

I know it's not nearly a good enough excuse to leave, but it is the truth. I had every intention of visiting you at first, but the more time passed, the harder it became to go back. I regret that now. If I could go back in time and do it all again, I would have done things differently. I would have tried harder. I would have fought for you. I'm so sorry I didn't.

When I found out your mother had remarried and you had a chance at having a real father, I used that excuse to justify my decision to stay away. Convincing myself that I had already done enough damage. Again, I was wrong. I realise that now.

Despite everything I did, your mother kindly sent me pictures of you over the years, which I cherished. I couldn't be prouder of the woman you've become.

A part of me always knew I'd be too much of a coward to tell you this in person. I'm hoping that while you're reading this letter, you're at the store, in Bluestone, and this isn't just something you found in boxes that were shipped over to you.

I left you the store in the hope that you might come here, Lily. Even if I'm long gone, I'd like to share at least one thing with you. Maybe you'll fall in love with it too? Maybe you hate the city like me and want to move here? Or maybe you'll sell it and never look back.

Whatever you do, Lily, I hope one day you can forgive me.

Tears pricked her eyes. Every inch of her wanted to hate him. Hate him for what he did, hate him for what he'd said, and most of all hate him for asking for her forgiveness. But his words had hit too close to home. His stupid ramblings about the city. They were the very same words she'd uttered to Jake on their second date. She couldn't ignore her own reflection in his letter. Even though she wanted to. Badly.

Doing everything she could to keep it together, she leaned over the bed to the side table where her phone rested. She was knee-deep in crap already, she might as well bite the bullet and call her mother.

Lily let her mother, who was surprised to hear from her, get her rant out of her system while she gathered her thoughts. This wasn't a social call, she needed answers. When the line finally went quiet, she took her chance.

"I just found something. A box of pictures of me and a letter that Dad left me." She heard her mother suck in a breath but continued. "I'm angry, I'm upset, but most of all I'm confused, Mum. I need you to talk to me, answer my questions and for once in your life, tell me the truth… can you do that? Or do I need to call you back in another month?" Her voice was deceptively calm, but inside she was screaming, crying and mentally throwing heavy objects around the room.

Her mother let out a heavy sigh. Lily could picture the furrowed brow she'd formed as she spoke again. "What do you want to know, Lily?"

"How did Dad know you remarried?"

The line went silent again for a moment. "Your father and I were in touch for a few years after he left. But when I married Steve, that ended."

"So why does he have photos of me up until I was eighteen?"

Lily heard a big huff down the phone. "Every year, on your birthday, I sent him a photo of you. But we didn't talk. It was just the photos. After you turned eighteen, it was up to him to seek you out if he wanted to."

"Did he ever call or write to say that he'd received them?" Trying to remain composed, Lily twisted the frayed edges of her denim shorts around her index finger.

"No. I just assumed he did. Other than the letters I sent back and a few phone calls up until I remarried, I've had no contact with him. After he found out about Steve, he just stopped calling."

"When he first moved here, did he try and come visit me at all? I know in one of the letters you sent back he mentioned a visit."

"Lily ..." Her mother's voice was unusually soft. "I know you're angry at me for sending those back, but I had my reasons. Your dad loved you, he did. But on the phone, he made it clear to me he had no intention of flying back to England. I offered to share custody, I even told him you could spend summers over there, but that's not what he wanted. I know it's hard to hear, hard to understand, but those letters would have only confused you. You were so young, Lily; I didn't want to give you false hope ..." She trailed off.

Guilt washed over Lily. Her mother was just trying to protect her. Tears dripped down her cheek, this time she couldn't stop them.

"He didn't want me," she whispered down the line.

"Darling." Her mother's voice cracked. "It had nothing to do with you. Do you hear me? You were perfect then and you're perfect now. If anything, I feel sad for your father, I always have, because he missed out on knowing you. Having you in his life. But we can't change the past Lily ... only the present."

She nodded as if her mum could see her. She was right. Neither of them could change the past. What was important was now.

***

Lily's eyes grew wider as Jake placed her plate down in front of her. Digging into the succulent steak and savouring every bite, she glanced up briefly to catch him grinning at her.

"What?"

"Nothing. You just look cute when you eat."

Flush crept up her neck. No boyfriend had cooked her such a romantic dinner before. When she'd first seen the candles adorning the table, she'd smothered her surprise. Still expecting Sam to walk in at any moment, it felt odd to have the place to themselves.

"You talk to your mom again?" Jake asked in between bites.

Lily had already told him about the letter and the call with her mother. He'd come straight over to see her when he heard and had spent the rest of the week checking in. He sure had a way of making her feel special.

"Yeah, she called this morning to see if I was okay." She took a big gulp of her wine before continuing. "As much as she drives me crazy, I do miss her. I'm glad things are okay between us now."

Jake reached over the table and placed his giant hand on hers. "Do you think she'll come out to visit you? I'd like to meet her."

Trust me, you don't mean that.

She shrugged. "I'm not sure about a visit, but she has made it very clear that she wants me back in London for Ali's birthday. But I don't know yet if I'm going to go."

"When's her birthday?"

"In a few weeks,"

Jake suddenly stiffened and moved his hand back.

"I don't know if it's very practical, what with the store and everything," Lily went on.

She watched as his attention turned back to his food,

wondering if she'd said something wrong. He'd gone from caring to cold in a matter of seconds.

"Everything okay?" she prodded but only received a nod. "Come on, Jake, what is it?"

"How long would you be gone for—if you went back?" He sighed, and she noticed his brow furrow.

"Um, I don't know, maybe a week or two. Why? Is that what's bothering you?"

Jake sunk back into the wooden chair and avoided her gaze. "I don't want you to go."

His comment caught her off guard. Was he asking her or telling her? Trying to decipher the sudden change in tone, she looked at him puzzled and waited for him to elaborate. When he finally met her eyes, she stared into the blue and green flecks catching the candlelight.

"Don't go," he repeated.

"I don't understand. Why not?"

"Because I'll miss you."

Now she really was confused. She didn't know whether to be flattered or concerned by the possessiveness lacing his tone. Before she had time to consider what he'd said, his expression shifted to smouldering and all rational thought escaped her. Mind muted, her body was now in control.

"You better stop looking at me like that, Lily, if you want to finish your dinner."

Rising from her chair, his eyes followed her around the table as she placed herself on his lap. A deep, sexy growl vibrated through him as he dragged her into his chest, capturing her lips and pushing her open.

Thrusting his tongue inside, he tasted every inch of her as liquid heat pooled in her stomach. Releasing her grip on his shoulders, she let her hands skate down his hard chest while his hands glided down her back. When he reached the waistband of her shorts, he pushed under her vest. Rough fingertips burned her skin and settled into the curve of her waist.

When their breathing became ragged and lack of oxygen

to the brain became a real concern, he released her lips and tracked soft kisses around her mouth and across her jawline.

"You could make a man lose his goddamn mind, sweetheart." His husky drawl only made her heart thump harder.

When he started to flick his tongue over her earlobe and down her neck, everything started to spin. She was hooked. Every touch, every taste, every smell. Everything about this man caused her body to pulsate. And as he rocked his hips against her, she knew she had to have him.

"I want you," she whispered through her gasps.

Jake's grip on her tightened as he stood, bringing her with him.

"Wrap your legs around me, darlin'." He smiled as he pulled her closer.

She did as he asked, thrilled and ridiculously turned on by the fact he could pick her up with such ease. Safely nestled in his arms, he carried her out of the dining room and up the stairs. With one kick, the door to his bedroom was open.

***

Lily let out another sigh as she tried again to focus on the monthly report. She was feeling extra claustrophobic in her office today, but she needed to get through this before she could see Jake.

Three weeks into being official and their relationship wasn't just confined to weekends anymore. They had quickly added weeknights, lunches and regular calls to their schedules.

Her thoughts wandered back to last night. Jake had surprised her by turning up with groceries and cooking up a feast while she soaked in the tub. For the first time in a long time, she felt content. There were no games and no drama. They had amazing sex, he phoned when he said he would, they talked about anything and everything, and he made her feel secure. Not only did he make her feel like the only woman in the world, but he also made her feel safe. Like if she gave him her heart, she could trust him with it.

You're finally in an adult relationship. Now don't fuck it up.

Occasionally her brain would still troll her and tell her it was too good to be true. In the past she would have let those kinds of thoughts consume her, but not this time. This time she was determined to enjoy it. She deserved happiness. She deserved to be treated right. God knows she had paid her dues.

Now, only if her monthly profit margins were as positive as her.

Nope, still not making any money.

Letting her head fall into her desk, she let out a frustrated groan. Eventually she picked herself up and dragged herself over to the coffee pot. Caffeine would help.

It was only when she'd practically inhaled every drop in her mug that she turned her attention back to her laptop.

Even though the web sales had helped, there weren't enough of them. Rob had sent her over a marketing plan that would help increase sales, but the upfront cost of the adverts was too much for her to consider right now.

What the hell am I going to do?

She was happy for the distraction when her phone beeped. And she felt herself smile as she saw Jake's name.

Jake: I miss you.

Profit margins could wait. She was ready to see her man.

She closed her laptop, then locked up the office. But before she could head upstairs to get changed, she heard a knock at the door.

Even better. He was here. She was so excited that before Jake had even uttered a word, she was in his arms and brushing her lips across his.

"Happy to see you too, darlin'," he muttered against her lips.

Once she found the willpower to pull herself away, she spoke. "What are you doing here? I thought I was coming over later?"

"I couldn't wait. I missed you." He tilted her chin up and took another taste of her lips.

She was in way over her head. She was a goner. He'd actually ruined her for any other man.

Please don't break my heart.

After fighting the urge to strip him in the street, she released herself from his clutches and tugged his arm until he was inside.

"Upstairs. Now."

His husky laugh echoed across the shop floor. "Yes, ma'am."

CHAPTER FIFTEEN

The first light of the day leaked in through a gap in the drawn curtains. Jake had woken before his alarm, but he couldn't quite bring himself to get up just yet.

Rolling his shoulders, he became acutely aware of his achy muscles. Despite their early night, not much sleeping had taken place, like every night they'd spent together over the past few weeks. But it didn't matter, he was more interested in familiarising himself with Lily's body. Something he would happily forgo sleep for any time.

Jake's gaze went back to the woman in question, who was still asleep. Her wavy, golden hair draped over her bare shoulder and brushed against the top of the sheet that was pulled over her breasts. He'd never seen anyone so beautiful. She had him feeling things he'd never felt before, and it scared the shit out of him.

At first he thought it might just be the thrill of the chase, and when they started to date he thought it must be the misplaced sexual tension, but now ... now he didn't have a clue. They'd scratched their itch over and over again, but that feeling was still there. If anything, it had gotten stronger. She was the first thing he thought about when he woke up and the very last thing that flashed through his mind before he slept. Even the sexual tension hadn't been dispelled. He couldn't get enough of her. He'd even considered hiring another ranch hand just so he could spend longer in bed with her.

When Lily started to stir, he lay still, hoping he wouldn't wake her. It was still early, and she needed her rest. It was her day off after all. He looked back at his clock; he'd have to start his chores soon. A part of him wanted to text Brodie and ask him to cover so he didn't have to leave her.

"Morning," she whispered hazily, one eye squinting open.

Her lush, honied skin called out to him, and he couldn't resist touching her. Carefully, he ran his fingers down her cheek, studying her lips as they gently parted. "You should be sleeping, darlin'; it's still early."

A smile as sweet as sugar formed, lighting up her emerald eyes, when she caught his hand as he stroked her. "But what if I'd rather be awake with you?"

Pulling her hand toward him, he ran his lips over her knuckles and stared into her until her cheeks started to pinken. He couldn't help but grin at the effect he had on her. Letting instinct take over, he tugged her into his arms and felt his blood pump faster as her smooth skin pressed up against his hardened body.

Taking his mouth to her ear, he felt her breathing become shallower. "And what would you like to do while you're awake with me, Lily?"

She gently dipped her head and planted soft, wet kisses along his neck. Already struggling to control himself, the graze of her teeth against his skin was too much for him to handle. Pulses of electricity coursed through his veins as he cupped her face and pulled her to his lips.

***

Predictably late for his morning chores, he gave in and messaged Brodie. Luckily, Lily had agreed to spend the whole weekend at the ranch, so even if he had to pitch in and help, he got to come back to the house and spend time with her afterward.

After eventually dragging himself away, he went to meet Brodie by the barn to help him exercise the horses.

Dodging Brodie's knowing laugh as he looked him up and down, he made his way inside to check on the horses.

"Late night?" Brodie winked at him as he escorted Rocky outside.

Ignoring the tone, Jake nodded. "Yeah, sorry, man. Thanks for covering. If you're interested in more hours, I could use help tomorrow as well."

"Oh yeah? How come?"

Jake didn't meet his grin and instead focused on Rocky. "Um … Lily's staying over, and it'd be good to spend a little extra time with her."

Brodie sniggered. "Damn." After letting out another deep laugh, he turned to look at Jake again. "Man, I've never seen you like this before. You're falling hard for this girl."

"So what if I am?" Coming out more defensive than he intended, Jake let a smirk soften his question.

"Well, I'm happy for you, man. Lily's a good girl. You're one lucky man," Brody said sincerely as he patted down their silver mare, Sunny.

Jake didn't know what to say to that. He wasn't used to having his love life discussed, probably because nothing lasted long enough for other people to catch wind of it. But Brodie was a good guy; he'd been with his wife, Laura, for five years now. If anyone was in a position to offer up any relationship advice, it was him.

"Can I ask you something?" Jake waited for Brody to nod before he continued. "How do you know if she's …" Feeling uneasy, he paused.

"If she's the one?" Brodie finished for him. "You just know. With Laura, I remember looking at her one morning and thinking, goddamn, I'm gonna marry this girl."

Just the memory widened Brodie's smile. There was no

doubt the man was crazy in love with Laura. There was that word again. Love. The word that had dangled on the tip of Jake's tongue for the last week. He still wasn't sure he knew what love was, so how was he supposed to know if he really was in love with her?

Once they'd finished with the horses, he headed back to the main house, already missing the taste of Lily's lips. A waft of smoky bacon hit him as soon as he came through the door, setting off a rumble in his empty stomach.

"Lily?" he called out as he followed the smell to the kitchen. "Are you doing what I think you're doing?"

She looked even tastier than the bacon as she cooked in nothing but his shirt.

"Hot damn, you look good in that, sweetheart."

A devilish smile formed on her face as she fluttered her eyelashes at him. "I hope you're hungry."

"Damn right I am." He couldn't get over there quicker. Slipping his hands around her waist from behind, he pressed into her and let his mouth suck and nibble until she broke into a fit of giggles. "How about we let all this food cool down for a bit?" he asked, as a new kind of hunger began to simmer.

Quickly spinning her around, he lumbered her into his arms and caught her lips. As she twined her hands around his neck, he knew he was done for.

"Bedroom. Now," he croaked out. Breakfast would have to wait; she was the only thing he was interested in tasting right now.

***

Missing the warm spring breeze, Jake felt his shirt cling to the sweat trickling down his back. He needed a shower and a cold beer. Kicking off his boots, he went for the beer first.

As he uncapped the bottle and took a long, refreshing swig, the melodic sound of Lily's voice caught his attention.

Following the sound toward the porch, he noticed the back of Sam's head first. The two of them were deep in conversation. A serious conversation by the looks of it.

A smile brandished his face. He couldn't wait to wrap his arms around Lily. But before he could launch himself at her, Sam's question stopped him in his tracks.

"What would you do, go back to live in London?"

They both went quiet, and he waited for what felt like an eternity for Lily's reply.

"I guess so … maybe … I don't know. I'm not sure I'd have a choice. I've nearly burnt through all my savings. It's only a matter of time now before I have to make a decision."

He felt a knot start to twist in the pit of his stomach. She was thinking about leaving. Leaving him. What the hell? After all her jibes about his commitment issues, now she was the one considering leaving.

What hurt the most was that she hadn't even told him. She was out there telling his sister instead. He could've helped. Been there for her. The fact she'd kept quiet spoke volumes. She still didn't trust him. He felt like an idiot.

Serves you right for falling for a city girl.

Unable to face her, he dragged himself away from the door and skulked up to the bathroom. He felt numb and even the cold, harsh sprays of the shower pounding his face couldn't bring the sensations back to his body.

After he'd towelled off, his brain seemed to switch back on and more questions started to surface. What happens next? He couldn't decide between confronting her or waiting for her to come to him, but he knew he needed to protect himself in case she did leave. It figures that after a lifetime of running away from women and relationships, he finally finds someone he wants to stand still with and then she runs. Karma was a bitch.

CHAPTER SIXTEEN

Jake was pulling away; she could feel it. They had hardly seen each other since her visit to the ranch last weekend, and when they had, he'd been unusually quiet and distant. They hadn't even spent the night together. She was trying her hardest not to overanalyse the coincidental timeframe of them sleeping together and then him pulling away. Sure, it had been a few weeks of sleeping together, but maybe that was what he did. He did say his longest relationship was two months after all. God, she felt like a cliché.

It was the regular ranch barbecue tonight, and although a part of her wanted to stay home, crawl into a ball and cry, she found her backbone and dragged herself over there.

Her stomach churned as she caught sight of Jake, deep in conversation with a very pretty guest. A pang of jealousy hit her. Was this why he was avoiding her? He'd found someone else, someone prettier, someone more interesting.

Stupid Lily. Look at him; he's gorgeous. Why would he want you when he can have her or any other woman? He's got what he wanted and now he's done. He's bored of you.

Her stomach churned; she was going to be sick. She quickly turned around and hurried back toward the house. But it was too late—she could feel the bile coming up. She managed to sprint around the house so she was out of view, and then instantly fell to the ground.

Tears streamed out along with the contents of her stomach. If she didn't feel like an idiot before, there was no doubt she felt like one now.

"Jesus, Lily. Are you okay?" Jake's voice rang out behind her, and within a second, he was on his knees, stroking her back. "You've been sick. Are you ill?"

No words were coming out anytime soon, so she just nodded.

"Come here." He pulled her to her feet and into his arms.

Resting her face in his chest, the tears continued to fall.

"It's okay, sweetheart. I'm gonna take care of you. Don't cry, darlin'—it's okay."

His sweet comfort only tore at her heart more. Maybe she was wrong. *Please, God, let me be wrong.* The feel of his fingers gently gliding up and down her spine managed to soothe her. It was a few minutes before she found her voice again. And when she did, she slowly unplucked herself from his hold and looked up to see the concern in his eyes.

"Do you think we could go inside? To talk?" Her voice shook.

Once they were inside, he continued his thoughtful caresses until she pulled away again. The instant she did, she felt the atmosphere change and tension start to crackle. As she dared to meet his eyes, she noticed the concern in his gaze had disappeared and had been replaced by something she couldn't quite identify.

"You wanted to talk, so talk." Jake's words were clipped, his tone almost detached. And it only made her feel sicker.

"I've umm … I've decided to go to London next week for Ali's birthday. I'm gonna shut the shop while I'm away."

"I thought you weren't going back for Alice's birthday?"

"No. You asked me not to go back. But I've decided to go." *Because I'm not a doormat. Not anymore at least.*

"Great. Another thing you forgot to tell me," Jake

snapped, the look in his eyes making her heart beat faster.

"What?"

"You heard me, Lily. So is this your idea of how a relationship is supposed to work? Us keeping secrets from each other?"

What the hell?

"I've not been keeping it a secret, Jake—you've been avoiding me all week … when exactly was I supposed to tell you?" She was doing her best to stay strong and fought back the tears bubbling.

"I've not been avoiding you, Lily."

"Oh really? So for the past week you haven't avoided spending the night with me or being alone with me for more than five minutes?"

His guilty expression said it all. "It's not like that, Lily— I've been busy."

"Bullshit. You're pushing me away."

Ignoring the trembling of her raised voice, she kept her eyes firmly on his.

"So what if I am? Why do you care? You're going back to London anyway. Evidently you got what you wanted."

"What the hell are you talking about?"

"You want me to spell it out for you?" His face was so cold she felt a shiver run down her spine. When she didn't reply, he carried on. "Fine. You come out here for some romanticised adventure from your boring life, you make some friends, fuck a local and then you're gone like this is some kind of fucking holiday resort and not people's real goddamn lives."

She took a moment to let his words sink in. Was he really doing this, saying this?

"Wow, Jake. Wow. So is this how you do it every time? Pick an argument and blame it on them?"

A harsh laugh escaped his lips before he stood. "You don't know what you're talking about."

Pushing away from the chair, she matched his stance, anger coursing through her veins. "Actually, Jake, I do. It's been two months, has it not? Well, *ding, ding, ding*, your timer must be up! It must be time to cut and run!" She stopped any words leaving his mouth with her hand. "Well, fuck you, Jake. Fuck you for convincing me I was different, fuck you for tricking me into bed, and fuck you for breaking my fucking heart!"

She didn't wait for a reply. She was done. She got out of there as fast as her feet could carry her and as fast as her car could skid along the gravel.

***

As soon as she arrived home, she started packing her suitcase and called the airline to change her ticket to the next available flight. She needed to get out of there now. Jake had already tried to call her and she hated the idea of him just showing up.

Within an hour, she'd loaded up her car, locked up the shop, and left Jessie a message telling her she would be out of town for a bit. It was a long way to the nearest airport; she had naively thought the drive would help her compose herself and her thoughts, but the more time went on, the worse she felt.

After trying to drown out all the self-deprecating insults her mind was throwing out at her with some angry rock music, she let out a sigh and turned it off. She'd been putting off calling Alice to ask for a lift from Heathrow, but she might as well get it out of the way.

"Hey, hey, hey, Lilypad, what's a cracking?" Alice's cheerful voice echoed out of the speakerphone.

"Hey, Ali, I'm just on my way to the airport. I'm getting an earlier flight—don't suppose you'll be around to pick me up tomorrow?"

"Sis?"

"Yeah?" Lily replied innocently.

"What's going on? And don't try and pull that 'it's nothing, I'm fine' crap on me."

Damnit. Nothing got past that girl. "I needed to get out of there, okay? It's only an extra couple of days anyway—it's not a big deal."

"You have a fight with loverboy?" Lily's silence obviously spoke volumes as Alice continued a moment later. "Come on, spill. What happened?"

"There's nothing to say, Ali. It's over, and no, I don't want to talk about it."

"Okay, we don't have to talk about it now, but you can bet your arse we'll be talking about it when you're back in London."

Lily rolled her eyes. "We'll see."

"All right, sis, text me your flight info and I will be there with bells on."

Once she'd hung up, she went back to feeling sorry for herself. Breaking up with Jake already hurt like hell, and she knew it was going to get worse.

The sting of pain stayed with her the rest of the journey and settled once again in her stomach as she sat in the airport waiting for her gate to board. Her phone rang out again, but this time it wasn't Jake, who had left her two more missed calls since she'd left her apartment.

After taking a very long, deep breath, she answered. "Hey, Sam."

"Jake said you had a fight. Are you okay? I went by the store and you weren't there. Where are you?"

Lily didn't know why she expected Sam to automatically side with her brother and cut her off too, but after hearing the concern in her voice, she suddenly felt childish for even thinking it.

"Umm … Jake and I broke up."

"What? You guys are over, for good? What happened, and where are you?"

"It's still a little raw right now, Sam. I, uh … I'm at the airport. You know I told you I was gonna go home for a visit next week? Well, I thought I would go back early, see my family and stuff."

"But what about the store and the web orders?"

"I've closed the store and I put up a notice on the site. After what happened with Jake, I just needed to get out of there. I'm sorry; I should have called you."

"Are you okay?"

"Not really. To be honest, I'm still processing it. Can we talk when I get back?"

The line went quiet for a bit until Sam finally replied. "Of course, Lily. You know I'm here if you need anything. When are you coming back? I mean, you *are* coming back, right?"

She hadn't forgotten their conversation last week, nor had Sam apparently. But like she told her friend then, Bluestone was her home now. It was where she was happiest. And she would do everything in her power to stay.

"I'm not moving back if that's what you're asking. I just need some time … to figure things out. I'll be back, I promise. I don't know when, but I will. And I'll keep in touch."

As she hung up, Lily felt like the weight of the world was on her shoulders. Talk about a bad day. The store still wasn't making a profit, Jake had compared their relationship to her "fucking a local" and her only friend in her new hometown was her now ex's sister. She had a lot of thinking to do.

CHAPTER SEVENTEEN

"What the hell did you do to her?" Sam stormed over to the barn and started to push on his chest.

After finding his balance again and restraining her hands, he faced his angry sister's glare.

"Calm the fuck down, Sam."

"What did you do to her? You promised me this was different. You lied to me, Jake. How could you?"

"Goddamnit, Sam, it was different. It *is* different."

"Yeah, then why is Lily on a plane back to London for God knows how long? She said you broke up. She shut the store and put a stop to her web orders."

She's on a plane? He wanted to punch something, kick something, drink something. He'd tried to call her after their fight, but she was obviously ignoring him, as her phone was evidently working if she'd spoken to Sam. How could she just leave like that?

Because you were an asshole to her. Because she was right—you have been pushing her away since you heard her conversation with Sam. Because you should have spoken to her about what you heard and not assumed the worst.

"Damnit. I need to talk to her. When is she coming back?"

"I don't know, Jake. Because of you, she might not want to come back. Now tell me what the hell happened from the beginning."

The idea of never seeing Lily again hit him like a punch to the gut. Had he really lost her for good? An onslaught of cursing from Sam commenced while he wrestled with what to do next. He needed a drink. Tuning his sister out, he made his way to the house. Unsurprisingly, Sam followed.

With a beer in hand and daggers in the back of his head, he took a seat at the kitchen counter.

"I fucked up, okay? Are you happy?"

"Far from it. What happened?"

"I heard you guys talking the other week about the store and her moving back to London."

Sam crossed her arms but didn't utter a word.

"I was pissed off that she was even considering going back."

"And? Did you talk to her about it?"

"No."

"You're a dumbass."

"You think it's okay she didn't tell me? Didn't talk to me? We are supposed to be in a relationship; we are supposed to talk to each other about everything. Why the fuck was she hiding shit from me? Last time I checked, moving to another goddamn country is a big fucking deal!"

"Why didn't you just talk to her?"

The last thing he needed right now was a lecture from his little sister. So instead of going into detail, he tried to shrug her off. "It doesn't matter now, does it? Once a city girl, always a city girl." Slamming his bottle down, he stood and headed for the door. But before he could get out of there Sam was in his face, tugging at his shirt.

"That's what this is about. Mom? Cos she left, Lily will too?"

"Calm down, Doctor Phil, don't start analysing me."

"Stop being such a stubborn asshole, Jake. I know you better than you think. I know you're scared as hell to let anyone in. Maybe it's cos of Mom, maybe it's not. But don't fuck it up with Lily cos you're scared. She deserves more than that. For God's sake, *you* deserve more than that."

Shoving past her, he stamped up the stairs and slammed the door of his bedroom behind him. Sam's words hit a nerve. Had his mother really fucked him up that much?

No, she was just an example of why it would never work out between us. Lily's from another country, from a city. She was just killing time with you until she got bored and went back home. She'd hate country life, just like your mom did.

"Goddamnit."

Jake picked up his lamp and smashed it against the wall.

***

Mickey's was packed. Even Mickey himself had made an appearance, much to Teddy's dismay. Whenever the old man was around, he'd spend his time micromanaging the bar staff until they all needed a big drink themselves.

Ever since Lily left, Jake had felt lost and had quickly returned to his old routine of nights in the bar. It gave him a chance to drown his sorrows as well as avoid Sam's wrath, which was still going strong. Luckily, word of his breakup with Lily hadn't hit the town gossip mill yet so he was left mostly alone, which is what he wanted.

After ordering another beer, Teddy took a break and joined him at his table.

"You gonna tell me what's going on?" Teddy's eyes narrowed on him.

"And what makes you think anything's going on?"

"Cos you've been nursing a beer every night this week, sittin' alone at this table, looking like it's the goddamn end of the world."

Jake let out a sigh. Little did Teddy know that Lily leaving had felt like the end of the world. "Just between us?" Jake waited for Teddy to nod. "I think Lily and I are done."

"Shit, man. I'm sorry. Is that why she's in London?"

Jake gave him an abbreviated version of what had gone down and waited for the inevitable "you're a dumbass" jab that Brodie and Sam had offered up.

"You love her?"

Who the hell knows? I'm probably not even capable of it. "I don't know. I'm not exactly an expert on this love stuff."

"Neither am I, but it's pretty simple. Did you ever see a future with her … marrying her?"

Jake shrugged, hoping Teddy would continue.

"What about living with her? Did you want to wake up with her every day, go to bed with her every night?" That one earned Teddy a nod. "And you think about her when you're not with her, wondering what she's doing, counting down the minutes until you see her?"

"And if I say yes to all of the above that means I'm in love with her?"

"How 'bout this one. When she left, how did you feel?"

"Pissed off. Nauseous. Like she'd ripped my goddamn heart out. I broke my fucking lamp." His mouth suddenly dry, Jake drained the rest of the bottle.

Teddy let out a snigger. "Spoken like a man in love."

"Fuck off, Teddy."

Teddy held up his hands in defence. "Listen, there ain't a love checklist or nothin', but come on, man, don't be blind. You think about her all the time, wanna see her all the time, and when she left you felt broken? Read the writing on the wall, man."

And with those wise words, Teddy stood and patted Jake's shoulder before heading back to the bar.

CHAPTER EIGHTEEN

Lily stared at the broken, grey clouds looming above them. They had been sitting in the beer garden of Alice's favourite pub for an hour now and she still wasn't feeling any better, despite her sister's best efforts.

"Another round?" Alice chimed from across the bench, snapping Lily out of her daydream.

She slumped over the table and lay her forehead against her folded arms. "Please take me home, Ali. I'm a miserable bitch, and I prefer to ugly cry in private."

"No fricking way, sis. You and I are gonna hash this out. Now, you keep your sad arse put while I fetch us some shots."

Lily let out a dramatic groan as she listened to Alice stand and take herself over to the bar. She finally lifted her head at the sound of glasses clinking.

"Don't you think ten shots are overkill?" She looked in horror at the pockets of dark liquid scattered across the metal tray.

"Nope, by the time we reach our fifth shot, I guarantee you'll be feeling a million times better."

"Yes, because drinking when you're sad always ends so well?" she sarcastically retorted.

Alice ignored her, placed the first shots in front of them and gestured for her to drink. They both sank it at the same time, probably pulling the same squeamish expression.

Alice clapped her hands, looking pleased with herself. "Right, let's get this shitfest started. So, loverboy turned out to be a fuckboy?"

The last thing Lily wanted to do was go over the story again, so she waited to see where this was going.

"Well, I say, fuck him. Fuck him and his fuckboy ways. Get your arse back there and show him what he's missing. Wear sexy clothes, flirt with his friends—hell, shag his bloody friends, just don't let that wanker ruin what you've built there."

That certainly wasn't what she was expecting to hear. "You're not gonna try and convince me to move back?"

"No fucking way—you were miserable here." Recognising her surprise, Alice grabbed her hand. "Look, Lily, I know I wasn't exactly the biggest supporter of you high-tailing it out of the country, but seeing you there ... I don't know. Seeing you so happy out there made me realise how unhappy you were here. Does that make sense?"

A rush of warmth ran through Lily as she offered Alice a smile. Lily didn't know if it was the shot, her sister's kind words, or the love in her eyes, but she didn't feel quite as hopeless as she did five minutes ago.

This time she placed a shot in front of Alice and gestured for them to drink.

After feeling the burn trickle down her throat, Lily was ready to talk. "Okay, Ali, my turn. Tell me the truth, what is it about me that attracts these types of men? Is it my clothes, my face, my personality—do I give off some kind of doormat vibe? You need to give it to me straight cos I can't keep having the same bloody relationship over and over again."

She watched as Alice's lips twitched, pondering her answer before squinting and letting out a sigh. "I don't think it's you, Lily. Maybe you're a little trusting, but that isn't necessarily a bad thing. You're a good person and you try and see the good in everyone." Another sigh left her mouth before she continued. "Honestly, I'm just as shocked as you about what happened with Jake. I saw the way he was with you, the way he looked at you ... and, well, if all he wanted was sex ... well, damn, we're all fucking screwed."

The sad truth was Lily was used to men disappointing her, over the years she had even become used to it, but having it happen with Jake had blindsided her. She'd spent the past week blaming herself, thinking she had some sort of gullible sign pasted across her back, so in a weird way she was glad Alice hadn't seen it coming either.

"Thanks, sis," she said as she dispensed the next round.

"Okay, Lilypad, my next bit of sisterly advice requires another shot, so get that fourth one down."

Lily's face spasmed as she sank the dark liquor and awaited Alice's words of wisdom.

"The store—you need to make some money if you're gonna stay in Bluestone. Rob told me about the website and thinks increasing online sales is the best chance of increasing your profit. And he said he's already worked up a marketing plan for you, which he is happy to implement free of charge."

"Rob's been amazing, but it's not just his expertise I can't afford, it's the adverts themselves."

"Yep, I know that. I wasn't done." Alice tipsily waved her finger at her. "It's cos you're trying to do everything all by your lonesome once again, Lily. Let me help you."

Lily opened her mouth to protest but her sister cut her off.

"Stop trying to interrupt me. Now, I'd give you the money in a heartbeat, but I know you wouldn't accept it. So, what I was thinking was that we could be partners ... business partners. I would be more of a silent partner cos I'll be here, but me buying into the business would give you enough money to grow it and draw a proper salary."

Lily took the last two shots from the tray and placed the

glasses in front of them.

"Are you serious?"

"Deadly." Alice beamed over at her. "So, was I right? By the fifth shot you feel better?"

For the first time in a week, Lily's smile hit her eyes. She lifted her glass and clinked it against her sister's. "To being partners."

***

Lily's mum took another long sip of her tea as her eyes roved over her. It was the first time they'd been alone in a week, and her mother's unusual silence was making her squirm. Trying to hide what an emotional wreck Lily had been, she'd spent all her time in London so far clinging to Alice.

"Ali mentioned you were going to be staying in town a bit longer. Is everything okay?"

She cleared her throat. "Um ... yeah. The store will be okay for a few weeks. When I get back, it's going to be a lot of work to get the online store set up so I don't have to do everything manually. Ali told you about what we're doing, right?"

After delicately placing her china cup on the oak table, Lily watched her mother smooth down her pristine pastel skirt. "Yes. I know all about you two going into business together. That's not what I meant. I wanted to know if you were okay, not the store."

No. Not even close. "Yeah. Why wouldn't I be?" She tried her hardest to plaster on a nonchalant smile.

"Lily Jayne Hart, don't you lie to me." Damn. Her mother only used her full name when she was in trouble. "You're still mad at me, aren't you? I know you've been avoiding me this week. I just don't know what else I can say, Lily. What can I do? Tell me what—"

"Mum, stop. It's not you, okay?" Feeling exasperated, she drained the rest of her smoky tea before she continued.

"I was seeing someone, and it ended. I just needed some time away, okay? Some time with my sister. And some time to regroup, so to speak."

"Oh, darling." Within a few seconds her mother had leapt and scurried over to wrap her arms around her. Lily let herself sink into her embrace, allowing the familiar citrus scent of her mother's perfume to soothe her. "You want to talk about it?"

Lily shook her head. There really wasn't anything else to say.

Her mother flopped onto the sofa next to her. "I'm proud of you, y'know? You picked up and left everything you've ever known and started again in another country. Running a business. Making new friends. All on your own. And even now, after having your heart broken, you're picking yourself up, holding your head high and going back to continue what you started."

Her jaw almost hit the floor, but before she could stammer out a "thank you," her mother held up her hand to stop her.

"You're a strong woman, Lily—there's no doubt about that. You always have been strong and independent. I admit, I relied on you a lot over the years … more than your sister. I didn't realise just how much until you were gone. I'm not too proud to admit that I was more than a little selfish in wanting you to come back home."

"Mum. You don't have to—"

"I do. Just let me get this out." She ran a hand over her perfectly styled blonde bob as if checking every hair was still in place. "I thought by keeping you close I was protecting you. Maybe I was trying to make up for what your dad did, or maybe I was scared of losing you too … I don't know. But somewhere along the way, it got skewered. I know that now. My attempt at keeping you close ended with you doing everything for me, even as an adult, I don't think there was a day that went by when I didn't speak to you. So when you left to do your soul-searching, I did some of my own too."

Lily felt a lump start to form in her throat, pushing any words back down as her eyes started to mist.

"You have your own life to lead, Lily. I know that now. Bluestone isn't exactly my first choice for you to lead it in, but as long as you're happy, that's all that really matters. That's all I've ever wanted."

Strong and independent. She'd never been called that before. Not by her family or her friends or by herself. The tears started to fall, and before she knew it, she was back in her mother's arms trying her best not to fall apart.

It wasn't long before words followed the tears and she found herself telling her all about Jake. She used to suffer in silence when it came to breakups, comforted normally by her good friends Ben and Jerry. A part of her felt pathetic feeling so broken by a two-month relationship; it's not like they'd been together two years. So why the hell did it hurt so much? Why was this harder than any other breakup she'd been through? And why did she feel so lost without him?

Almost as if her mother had read her mind, she mopped up the tears on her face with a tissue. "He's different, isn't he, from the other guys?" After a silent nod, her mum gently tucked her hair behind her ears. "Do you love him?"

And with that one question, back came the nausea.

CHAPTER NINETEEN

Beer wasn't enough tonight. Jake grabbed the bottle of whiskey he'd been saving and slouched back into the couch. After downing two shots, he measured out three fingers in his lowball glass and stared back at the screen. But it wasn't the game that had him so lost in thought. Like every night for the past three weeks, since Lily had left, she was the only thing that was on his mind.

A bang from the front door jolted him back to reality and reminded him to take another slug of his drink.

"Moved on to whiskey?" Sam glared as she leaned against the wall. A grunt was all he could muster as he turned his attention back toward the television. "Listen, Jake, there's something you should know. She's back. Lily's back."

His body reacted first, slamming the glass onto the coffee table as he pushed up from the couch and onto his feet. "She's here? At the store?" His heart started to pound. "I need to see her."

Heading straight for the hall, he sought out his boots, but before he could reach for them, Sam snapped his arm and pulled him back. "No, Jake. I'm not gonna let you do this. You need to give her some space."

"Like hell I do! She's had three weeks of goddamn space." He tugged his arm free and picked up his boots.

"I'm serious, Jake. She doesn't want to see you."

"She told you that?"

"Yes."

He froze and let Sam stare as his mind raced. And then panic set in. "Tell me she's not moving back to England?"

The dull ache in his chest started to spread across the rest of his body as he impatiently waited for his sister to reply.

"Come on, let's go back to the couch and talk."

"Not until you say it, Sam. I mean it."

"I don't know, Jake. Okay? She didn't say. Now come on."

Sam made sure he was seated again before she went into the kitchen to get herself a glass. After she'd poured out a shot, she turned down the game and sat on the chair next to the couch.

"So, you've seen her? Did she mention me at all?"

What, are you a teenager now?

"Yeah, I saw her. Before you start asking me a million questions, let me say my peace, okay?"

He bit his tongue and managed a nod.

"You hurt her, Jake. Like really hurt her. I don't know what her plans are, but maybe you should give her some time to settle back in before you go storming over there."

"No offence, Sam, but this is none of your business." He wasn't about to let his sister meddle again; he needed to see her.

"Okay, fine. What's your plan, Jake? Bang on her door and demand she hear you out? Come on, tell me, you're gonna go over there and say what to her?"

Enough. He was done with this conversation. This time when he got up, his sister knew better than to stop him.

***

Jake had been banging on the shop door for a solid fifteen minutes. He'd tried to call Lily's cell phone, but she'd turned it off. He knew she was there. Why was she doing this? Out of ideas, he called the only person who could possibly help.

"Where the hell is she, Sam?"

"Your bright idea not going to plan?" she chastised.

"Tell me where she is," he demanded.

"What, so you can go all caveman on her? I don't think so, Jake. Now get your dumb ass back here before someone calls the sheriff."

He slumped against the door as he hung up. He wasn't ready to give up. If she was upstairs, then she would hear him. He would make her hear him, even if it meant camping out here.

"I'm not going anywhere, Lily. I'll wait out here all goddamn night if that's what it takes!" he shouted up toward the window above the shop and banged against the door again.

In between banging, he texted her the same thing in the hope she would turn her phone on. He used the extra time to think about what he was going to say. His sister had been right to assume he didn't have a clue. All he knew was that he had to see her. Three weeks of not seeing her had made him crazy.

Two hours later, he let out a sigh as he checked his phone again. He was beginning to think that maybe Lily wasn't home. Just as he was about to throw in the towel, a light flicked on behind him. Quickly turning toward the door, he got his first glimpse of her. Dressed in her pearl white satin shorts and camisole, she looked like an angel as her golden tresses framed her face. God, he'd missed her.

As the door creaked open, he could see the apprehension in her eyes. He stayed quiet as he drank her in and resisted the urge to pull her into his arms.

"You need to go home, Jake." Her voice was quiet but calm.

"Not until we talk."

"It's late. Let's not do this now. Go home."

His pulse quickened, and he couldn't think straight. "Please, Lily. Can I come in?"

She shook her head, but he didn't see anger in her eyes, only sadness. The idea that he had been the one to put it there ripped him to shreds.

"Will you let me apologise to you at least? And explain?"

"I don't need some 'it's not you, it's me' fucking apology, Jake. I'm a big girl. I'll get over it." Attempting to mask her vulnerability, she defiantly crossed her arms and took a step back.

"Well, I won't get over it. And it was me, Lily—I fucked up. I thought that you were leaving. Leaving for good, and I was annoyed, and I was angry ... I should have talked to you—"

"Enough, Jake." Her voice rose, but when his gaze met hers, he realised that her mask had slipped, and he could see pain. "I can't do this right now. Please. Please, Jake. I want you to go."

A frustrated sigh escaped his lips. The last thing he wanted to do was go home. But the way she was looking at him was breaking his heart. She wasn't ready to hear what he had to say.

"I'll go." He pushed his hand through his hair and stumbled back. "But I'll be back tomorrow, Lily, to finish this conversation."

She closed the door without a reply. He waited until the lights were off before he moved again.

***

The next day, he finished off his morning chores and drove straight to the store. To his relief, it was open. Once he'd pushed through the door, he scanned the floor for her, but she was nowhere to be seen.

"Hey, Jake." Jessie cheerfully appeared in front of him.

"Hey, Jess. Lily around?"

"Umm ... no. She'll be out of town for a few days, said she had business in the city. She didn't tell you?"

His heart sank. Not just because she wasn't there but that she had business in the city. There was only one reason she would venture there. She was planning on selling the store.

No, no, no, no, no. How have you managed to fuck this up so badly?

He needed to fix this, but he didn't know how yet. His frustration must have been visible as he caught Jess's smile quickly flatten.

"She'll be back on Thursday, Jake. It's my day off, so she'll be in the store all day. Maybe try then?"

At least she won't be able to run away if she's manning the store. It also gave him a few days to figure out what he was going to do and how he was going to convince her to stay.

After thanking Jess, he slipped out.

CHAPTER TWENTY

It might make her a coward, but leaving town after seeing Jake again seemed like the best idea at the time. She'd needed to go to Billings anyway to visit the distribution centre, so it wasn't just like she was running away, at least that's what she told herself.

Who are you kidding? You're a total coward, Lily.

After loading up on vending machine snacks, she pulled the scratchy motel sheets over her and snuggled in to watch TV for the second night in a row.

An hour in and high on sugar, reality television was no longer keeping her attention. All she could think about was Jake. He looked so damn good when he'd turned up. How was she supposed to get over him when he went around looking all sexy and buff?

She knew it was only a matter of time before he tracked her down again and forced her to hear his apology. But the thought of hearing his polite breakup speech was too much for her to handle right now. The last thing she wanted to do was act all mature and pretend everything was fine, so until she was ready to return to the friend zone she would need to try her best to avoid, avoid, avoid.

Saved by the bell. Her phone rang out before she could

obsess further.

"So, how did the visit go?" Her sister's excitement had her grinning.

"What kind of greeting is that, Ali? Where's my, 'Hey, sis, you okay? How you doing today?'"

"All right, princess, how are you today? Oh, and when you're ready, take that tiara out of your arse and tell me what the fuck happened at the distribution centre."

Lily snickered. Her sister had such a way with words. "Okay, okay, don't get your knickers in a twist. It went well. It's the perfect space, and they've given us a good deal. They've agreed to a flexible start date depending on sales, but we need to give them a minimum of two weeks' notice. Seems fair."

Alice let out a squeal. "Fucking A. Right, Rob is ramping up ads, so how long, realistically, do you think you can do the distribution in-house?"

Lily peeled open another peanut butter cup while pondering. "Let's see how sales are the first week. If it gets too much, I will give Vince a call and get the ball rolling. But I reckon two weeks in-house will be fine. Jess will help, and I can ask Sam too."

"Cool. This is gonna work. I know it, Lilypad."

"Thanks, Ali. For everything. I don't know what I would do without you." If she'd learnt anything over the past few months, it was that a supportive family was much more important than a perfect one.

"Now don't you go getting all soppy on me, sis. You're too far away for me to bring you shots."

That earned her a laugh. "After three weeks of drinking with you, Ali, I don't ever want to look at another shot again. I'll be doing the adult thing and eating my feelings instead."

"Speaking of eating your feelings ... you seen him yet?"

"Yeah. I literally ran away. Skipped town the next day and came here."

"You're still in Billings?" Alice tutted. "Lily, you can't

hide forever. What did he say when you saw him?"

"There's not really much to tell." Lily fiddled with the sweet wrappers on the bed. "I didn't give him a chance to say much of anything. All he said was that he wanted to apologise. I told him to go home, and I came here the next day."

Alice went quiet for a bit while Lily continued to rustle packets. "You need to hear him out. The sooner you listen, the sooner you'll be able to move on."

She felt herself wince. Just seeing him again was painful enough. How on earth was she supposed to listen to his rejection without falling apart all over again?

***

At 8 a.m. she paced the flat while she brewed coffee. Today was the day. She knew that he would be back, and she had finally come to terms with the fact she would need to hear him out. Makeup and clothes were her armour. She'd spent extra time getting ready so she could at least not feel like utter rubbish when he launched into his 'it's not you, it's me' speech.

By 9 a.m., the door was unlocked, and the open sign was on full display. Unfortunately for her so were her shaky hands from too much caffeine.

Fuck.

By 11 a.m., there was still no sign of Jake, but she'd managed to dust all the shelves, disinfect the counter and wipe down the till. Still feeling on edge, she retrieved her laptop from the office and decided to check on the web sales.

Four web sales and two real-life customers kept her busy until noon. Once she'd packaged the orders, she decided to walk to the post office to burn off some of her anxiety. After putting up her back in ten sign, she locked up and made her way over.

Thankfully, the walk helped, and the caffeine shakes

finally subsided. Upbeat music blasted into her headphones while she gave herself an inner pep talk, all that with a trip to the café to pick up lunch was enough to lift her mood.

But then she saw him. Slouched against the store entrance, his gaze was firmly fixed on her as she crossed the street. Her stomach churned and all those reassuring voices in her head that had been so helpful five minutes ago, had vanished.

Shit.

Headphones out. Outfit checked. She unclasped her lip and tried to mentally prepare herself before she reached him. Even as she stood in front of him, he continued to stare, his eyes roving all over her. But there was no indication what was going through his head.

"Lily. Hi."

She managed to croak out a very quiet "hi" before unlocking the door and gesturing him inside.

Once in the store, she didn't know where to go. Should she just stand in the middle of the entrance? *No, that would be weird.* Should she go behind the till? *Yes, maybe.* In the end, the counter won. There was no harm in putting distance between them. But before she could reach the safety of the partition, his strong hand gripped her shoulder and spun her around.

"Please don't run away again, Lily."

She stuttered a half-arsed reply about just going behind the till as he inched closer to her. Feeling the warmth of his breath hit the top of her forehead and his intoxicating scent fill her lungs, she was almost too scared to look up. Like always, the rough edge of his fingertip made the decision for her as he tilted her chin upwards until their eyes locked.

"I'm so sorry, Lily. I fucked up. Will you let me explain what happened?"

Her lips parted but no words came out. So she nodded to indicate he could continue.

"I overheard you talking to Sam about moving back to London ... for good. I was pissed as hell. You hadn't even talked to me about it, and I felt like I wasn't even a consideration."

"Jake—" Her attempt at protest was swiftly shut down.

"Please just let me get this out." She let out a sigh as he carried on. "You were right; I was pushing you away. I figured that if you were going to be leaving, then I needed to protect myself and try to stay away from you."

She couldn't believe what she was hearing. A familiar ache in her chest resurfaced as she recognised the anguish in his eyes.

"I know it's no excuse for being an asshole, but I don't know ... maybe it goes some way to explaining it. I'm so sorry, Lily. I should have just come to you. Talked to you." He gently ran his knuckles across her cheek, down to her jaw. "But I'm here now, and I'm hoping it's not too late."

"Too late for what?" Her heart started to pound.

His stare intensified. "I'm all in, Lily. All fucking in. Whatever you decide to do about the store, we will make it work. If you want to sell and go back to London, then we can do long distance for a bit—just until I find cover for the ranch, and then I'll come find you. Move there. Get a job there. Or if you wanna stay here, then I can help you with the store, or you can move in with me and I'll take care of you. We can make this work; I know it."

What the fuck is he talking about?

"I don't understand. You want to move to London with me?"

"Lily, I'll follow you to Timbukfuckingtu if it means I get to be with you. I'm in love with you. I've fallen in love with you, Lily. I can't lose you. I *won't* lose you."

Her breath caught and her mouth went dry. He was in love with her? Her head automatically dropped, but within seconds, his hands clasped each side and pulled her gaze back to his.

"You're in love with me?" was all she managed to say as she looked at him in shock.

"Head over fucking heels."

The next thing she knew, his mouth was on hers and frantically prying her lips apart. Everything started to spin as the heat radiating off him prickled down her spine. Every sweep of his tongue reminded her of how much she'd missed him, his touch, his taste, his scent, all the things he made her feel.

She pushed back on his chest as she came up for air. After his hands dropped to her waist, she slid her fingers up to cup his face. "Jake … I love you too." Her breathing was still ragged, but she needed to get this out. "I'm not going anywhere. Not back to London, not to Timbuktu. I'm home."

His face lit up and his smile widened. She was more than ready to refamiliarize herself with the taste of his lips, but before she could snatch his mouth, he had slipped from her fingers. Within seconds, the front door was locked and the back in ten sign was reinstated. A sense of urgency flickered across his face as he strode back toward her, and in the blink of an eye she was off the floor and pressed against his chest.

"Jake, what the hell are you doing?"

"Making up for lost time."

***

After bringing down the last of her stuff, she joined Jake downstairs as he loaded up the truck. Apparently "all fucking in" meant moving in, and she was more than happy to take the next step. No more living in fear. It was time to trust herself and trust Jake too.

She was getting the best of both worlds: a hot man she loved in her bed every night and her best friend down the hall. Well, at least when Sam wasn't at Duke's.

Jake pulled her into him and tracked kisses up the nape of her neck until he reached her ear. "You ready for this, darlin'?" he whispered as he kept her steady in his arms.

"All in." She smiled as she angled her face to kiss him. And that's when she realised the past didn't matter anymore. Everything that had happened, good and bad, had led her to this moment. This perfect moment. A chance to start again and a chance to be happy. That was when she decided to forgive her dad. It was time.

EPILOGUE

Lily and Jake snuggled on the baby pink couch. As her gaze swept around the room, she knew without a doubt that this was the right decision. Duke sat on the matching pink armchair with Sam in his lap while her sister, Alice, continued to glare daggers at Jake's childhood best friend, Brady, as she leaned against the heart wallpaper that lined the chapel lobby.

When Jake had slipped a diamond ring on her finger a few weeks ago, neither of them wanted to wait any longer to make it official. They had spent their whole lives waiting for each other and didn't want to waste another second of it not being married. He was her forever. It had been six months since they'd moved in together and every day she fell a little more in love with him.

They both wanted a small wedding. As long as her sister was present, Lily didn't care about anyone else. So when Jake suggested Vegas, it seemed like a no-brainer. There she was, waiting her turn in the love chapel, still waiting for the nerves to come, but they didn't.

Jake's hand squeezed her hip as he motioned his head toward Alice and Brady. They were at it again.

"Maybe if you weren't such an arsewipe to the

receptionist we wouldn't have to wait so long," Alice sneered as Brady stalked toward her with a face like thunder.

Alice and Brady's hostility hadn't gone unnoticed. They'd met each other mere hours ago and had quickly gone from polite greetings to mortal enemies in the space of minutes. It was definitely out of character for her little sister; she had yet to meet any man she couldn't wrap around her little finger. That was until Brady. And from what she'd learnt about Brady over the past month since he'd moved back to Bluestone, he was pretty damn likable. Some would even say laid back. So seeing Alice bring out the beast was more than a little shocking.

"Do me a favour, darlin', and shut that pretty mouth of yours. You're ruining the goddamn moment." Brady braced his hand against the wall, next to where Alice's head rested, and crowded her.

Lily let out a snort as she watched her sister narrow her eyes and puff out her chest. She was getting ready for another battle.

"How about you do me a favour and back the fuck up before I knee you in the balls."

Even with just the side view of Brady's face, she could see the smirk. "What time is your flight back to London again, sweetness?"

Lily pondered whether now was the time to let everyone know that her recently-single baby sister wasn't going back to London. She was going back to Bluestone with them. Indefinitely.

DON'T MISS THE SECOND BOOK IN THE BLUESTONE SERIES:
Expiry Dating

Chapter One

Alice stared down at her phone in horror.

"No, no, no. This cannot be happening. Goddamn lying, cheating, son of a bitch."

Her phone was never going to survive this. Truthfully, as soon as she clicked on the picture, it never had a chance. A loud thud echoed around the room after it went flying through the air and crashed against the dark wood walls of her cabin.

It had been six months since she'd caught her ex-fiancé in bed with her best friend. Two months since she had quit her job. And one month since she'd begged her sister Lily to let her come stay with her on her ranch in Bluestone County. She had enough self-awareness to admit she was running away from her problems. But being in London right now wasn't an option. And after just seeing her ex-best friend's latest social media post it was a good thing she was in another country, or she would be locked up for grievous bodily harm.

"Oh my God Ali, what the hell did you do to your phone? The screen is all cracked!"

She hadn't even heard Lily come in. She was checking on her again, she'd been doing that a lot.

"Um… yeah, it fell. Don't worry, I'm sure I can get it fixed in town."

Lily's jade eyes narrowed, "oh really? And where exactly did it fall from Ali? The sky? Cos from where I'm standing it looks like it either magically fell from the ceiling or you threw it across the room in a fit of rage?"

This is the problem with being so close to your sister. She knows me too damn well.

Letting out a sigh, Alice slumped further down into the leather armchair that had been cocooning her for the past hour.

"Fucking Becky." She grumbled, "Apparently she's pregnant. I'll give you three guesses as to who the father is."

And there it was. Pity. All over her big sister's face.

"Oh Ali. I'm so sorry. How did you find out?"

"My friend forwarded me a post Becky made."

Lily closed the distance between them and took a hold of her hand, quickly pulling her up from the chair. "Come on. Let's go up to the main house. We can drink some wine, eat a fuckload of chocolate and plot revenge."

Alice reluctantly followed. Wine and chocolate were probably the only things that could possibly salvage today.

They were just a two-minute walk from the main house where Lily and her husband Jake lived. Jake's sister Sam used to live there too but had recently moved in with her boyfriend Duke.

Lily had initially wanted Alice to stay in the house with them, but she wanted the newlyweds to have some privacy.

That and she needed her own space too. Luckily, the ranch had guest cabins, so she was able to take up residence in one of them until she figures out her next move.

As they walked into the house and made their way into the spotless stainless-steel kitchen, a familiar voice pricked up the hair on the back of her neck.

No. Please don't be here right now. Please not today of all days.

Damnit. There he was. Brady. All six foot two of him. The new bane of her existence. In a fitted, tan, cop uniform so sexy it should be illegal. If she didn't already know he was the devil she could easily be fooled by his dark, brooding good looks. Even his damn caramel-coloured eyes were mesmerizing.

Mesmerizing eyes? Get a frigging grip Alice. He's the devil remember.

It had been three weeks since they'd first met in Vegas at Lily and Jake's impromptu wedding and despite trying to avoid him like the plague, he just kept showing up. Yes, Bluestone was small, and she was staying at his best friend's ranch, but it was actually getting ridiculous. He was everywhere. Whenever she ventured out whether it was to get coffee or go shopping, he was there. Waiting in the shadows, ready to make her life miserable.

"Looking good sweetness" Brady smirked as he purposely knocked her on the way over to the fridge, where he swiftly removed a beer bottle.

Alice shot him a glare over her shoulder, "Wish I could say the same to you Brady, but it appears as if the rumours really are true, and beer does go straight to a man's gut."

COMING SOON!

ABOUT THE AUTHOR

Isobel was born and raised in London. She still lives along the River Thames with her husband and her substantial book collection. Ever the hopeless romantic, she fell in love with the genre from a young age and was inspired to write her own stories. When she's not feasting on romantic comedies or binge reading her hoard of contemporary romance novels, Isobel is writing.

https://www.facebook.com/isobelreedbooks
https://www.instagram.com/isobelreedbooks/
https://www.isobelreed.net/
https://www.amazon.com/author/isobelreed
https://www.goodreads.com/Isobel_Reed
https://www.bookbub.com/authors/isobel-reed